Clair Huffaker was born in Ut
served in the Navy during Wo
South Pacific and after the wa
student at Princeton and then
in New York. Before going or
continental universities Huffak
and wrote for both *Time* and
return to New York he edited several magazines
at one time before becoming a freelance writer.

Author of over 200 short stories, numerous feature
and magazine articles, bestselling novels and
screenplays, Huffaker has also written for such
television series as 'Rawhide', 'The Virginian'
and 'Bonanza', and no less than seven of his
novels have been made into major motion pictures.

# Also by Huffaker

# CHAPTER ONE

An old mule with thick white hair in its ears first became aware of the approaching rider. It raised its tail and hee-hawed explosively, then took a swinging one-legged kick at a small bay mare who wandered over to see what the commotion was.

The half-dozen Rangers in the Devil River camp glanced up and saw a horseman top a rise two hundred yards away. He came on down toward the eight dirty gray tents lined raggedly near the river, letting his big blue roan pick her own way. He had no moustache, not even the beginnings of a masculine handlebar such as decorated the upper lip of each man in the camp, and his face was set in a constant half-smile, as though he was welcoming everything in the world to be his friend.

One Ranger, playing poker with two others, spat expertly, missing the edge of the blanket by the two inches that good form demanded. 'God p'serve us all,' he muttered. 'I'll bet three dollars that there is Smith.'

'In my opinion,' a second said quietly, 'they ain't got money down to Austin to pay this month's wages. First they send us Herly. Now they send this kid. They are prob'ly figuring all the fellas in Company D will now blow their brains out.'

The third card player shrugged. 'Who's raisin'? Maybe he ain't green as he looks. It ain't hardly possible.'

Entering camp, the young horseman reined up a few feet from a Ranger sewing a torn girth. 'This D Company?'

The man glanced up and scratched his chin with the big needle. 'Yep.'

'I'm Smith. Captain Bledscoe sent me up out of Austin.'

'Yeah.'

'Lieutenant Herly around?'

'Nope.' The man leaned back over the girth. 'See Sergeant

Hennesey. Tent at the end. And don't ride that horse through camp.'

Smith swung down and tied the roan, half-hitching the reins carefully to the branch of a smoke tree. Passing the card players on the blanket, he said pleasantly, 'Afternoon, boys.'

In the last tent he found a big burly man seated on a folding chair, laboriously writing on a pad in his lap.

'I'm Smith. You Sergeant Hennesey?'

The burly man glanced up, quick eyes darting from under thick eyebrows. 'Heard you comin'. You got the noisiest feet in West Texas.' He noted the tall young man's wide sloping shoulders and slimming waist and hips, his blue innocent eyes and laughter-lined face. 'How the hell old are you?'

'Twenty.'

'Well, don't jus' stand there. Lean on the tent pole or sit on the ground or somethin'.'

Smith sat on his heels and tipped his wide gray hat back on his head, and Hennesey dropped his writing pad on a bedroll.

'Got your papers?'

Smith handed the sergeant a folded envelope. Hennesey took two sheets of paper from it and spread them out before him in his big hands. 'Been in the Rangers nine days?'

'Yes, sir.'

'Jus' plain yes'll do it. How came you by the name of Seven, Smith?'

'Pa didn't wantta bother with fancy names. So he called us by the number of our comin'. There was One, and Two, and Three, and so on up to Thirteen. I was Seven. But Ma liked fancy names, so she always prettied 'em up a little.' Seven shifted his weight back and sat on the ground at the tent opening, legs crossed before him. 'Oldest boy was One for the Money. The next one was Two Hot to Handle. My honest-to-God name is Seven Ways From Sundown. But Seven is shorter.'

Hennesey slowly shook his head. 'You ask for duty out westward here?'

'Nope. They just told me to come on out.'

6

Hennesey studied the second of the two papers. 'You ever done any kind of fightin'? Commanche, maybe? Or Mex raiders, while me and Lee was off losin' to the Yankees?'

Seven shook his head. ' 'Fraid not.'

The sergeant stood up and scratched the handlebar moustache that was surrounded by two weeks of beard. 'Can you shoot them two Colts you're apackin'?'

Seven stood up with Hennesey. He hesitated. 'Well, I'm learning.'

'Come on out and let's have a look-see.'

At the edge of the camp Hennesey pointed to a small tip of rock jutting out of the Devil River a hundred and fifty feet from where they stood. 'Get them guns out as fast as you can and damage that rock as best you can.'

Seven pulled his guns and aimed with his right hand held straight out before him. He emptied one cylinder, switched guns and fired two rounds from the second revolver.

Hennesey touched him on the shoulder and said, 'That's enough. Son, I've seen old ladies draw buckets of water faster'n you drew them guns. And a fella sittin' on that rock woulda' been in the safest place in the river.'

Seven's face reddened as he began to reload. 'I'm better with a rifle. I'll learn quick.'

'You better, or you'll die quicker. You can bunk with James in the tent next to mine. Herly'll be back from Sonora sometime t'day.'

Seven took the furniture off his roan and hobbled her with the other animals. He took his warbag to the tent where he found a young man whom he guessed to be James sleeping on the south side. After quietly arranging his bedroll on the north side of the small cubicle of canvas, he heard a low, building sound of hoofbeats from outside, and left the tent to see who was coming. Two horsemen rode in at a lope and swung down from the horses at the edge of camp. Leaving their mounts ground-reined, they hurried to the last tent, where Hennesey was writing, ignoring the Rangers they passed on the way. A moment later one of the two men came back out of the tent and a Ranger said, 'Hey, Dagget, what's the fuss about?'

7

Dagget walked to the others and said, 'Two things, Carson. First, Jim Flood got outa Yuma Prison over in Arizona. Second, a Comanche war party hit Hatcher's farm. Stole two cows and a pig and wounded one a' Hatcher's boys. Dagget struck a match to a stub of cigar jutting out from under his moustache. 'We're agoin' after the Comanche, then Jim Flood.'

Carson grunted. 'How long ago'd he make his break?'

''Bout a week.'

'Never hear tell of a fella busin' outa' Yuma,' another said.

Dagget snorted, 'Just 'cause it's impossible, don't mean Flood can't do it. He prob'ly kicked a hole through them thick stone walls and walked out plain and simple.'

The second man who had ridden in appeared at the opening of Hennesey's tent and called, 'Dagget. Send the new man in here. The rest of you, except Jagers and Hoyt, get ready to move out fast.'

Dagget glanced at Seven and said, 'Reckon you're Smith.'

'Yeah.'

'Go see what Herly wants.'

Herly was sitting in the folding chair. He was a slender man with jet black hair and a small, thin moustache that was neatly trimmed.

The officer's eyes were bleak and wintery as gray ice. 'We will be leaving directly to punish a band of hostiles, Smith.'

'Yes.'

'Address me as sir. Get ready to travel.'

'Yes, sir.'

Within five minutes the six men going with Herly were in saddle. The lieutenant was the last man to mount. He turned his horse and started out of camp at a quick walk, the others falling in behind him.

Hennesey allowed his mount to drop back to where Seven was riding at the end of the irregular column. He looped his reins over the pommel and stuck his hands in the pockets of his jacket, sitting at a comfortable slope in the seat. 'They

8

put ya' to work right away, every time. Man's a damnable fool to join the Rangers.'

Smith grinned at him and nodded. 'How many Comanches are there?' His voice broke slightly, and he cleared his throat.

'If they was at Hatcher's place long enough to swipe two beefs and a hog, and only hurt one fella some, they ain't a very fearful outfit. Hatcher couldn't fight off more'n two squaws and a mean dog all at the same time.'

They rode northeast until the sun was down. At a fork in a small canyon Herly hesitated briefly, then started around to the right.

Hennesey grunted softly as his mount edged around to follow the others. 'Well, Seven, you are goin' to get the chance to meet Herly's girl. We'll be headin' by Harrington's Tradin' Post.'

Shortly after nightfall was complete, they rode down out of the hills and moved toward a dimly-lighted trading post. When they were a few hundred feet away a dog barked and the lights blinked out. They went on a moment after Herly stood in the stirrups and called out, 'It's all right, Harrington. I'm Lieutenant Herly with some of my men.'

The moon came over a ridge to the left and Seven could see an old man standing on the front gallery of the building with what looked like a double-barreled shotgun under one arm. 'Welcome,' the man called back. 'Come to supper.'

Herly told Seven to feed and water the horses in the barn behind the post, while the others went in to eat. When Seven had taken care of the mounts, he went into the post. The main part of the building was one large room surrounded by shelves and piles of goods. A plank table had been set up on two sawhorses in the center of the room and the Rangers had about finished eating.

Horses are tied out front,' Seven said.

'Took you long enough,' Herly grumbled. 'Getting short on time.'

'It won't take but a minute to feed that other man,' a light feminine voice announced through the door to the kitchen

9

at the far end of the room. Almost immediately a blonde, smiling young girl hurried out carrying a tray. 'I kept this on the stove for you. You must be new with Company D.'

'Yes, Ma'am.' Seven took off his hat and sat down uncomfortably, glancing apologetically at Herly.

Hennesey said, 'Seven Smith, it's your pleasure to meet Joy Harrington, and her old man Hap Harrington.'

Joy smiled and the owner of the trading post nodded from where he was standing behind a short counter, the shotgun still crooked under his arm.

'Pleased to make your acquaintance, miss,' Seven said.

'That's a nice name, Seven,' Joy decided. 'Sounds lucky. I'll get hot coffee for you.'

Hap Harrington spoke from behind the counter. 'Where you figure you'll catch them thievin' redskins, Herly?'

'If Smith ever finishes stuffing himself, I plan to find them around Cat Tail Flat.'

Seven ate quickly and was almost done when the girl came from the kitchen with coffee. 'I'm much obliged, miss,' he told her, 'but maybe I ought not take time for coffee.'

'All right. Come back for it another time.'

'Thank you.'

As they rode away from the trading post, Hennesey once more fell in at the rear with Seven. He said softly, 'That girl's got her eye on you.'

'She was just bein' nice.'

'There was an invite for you to come back for coffee.'

'She's Herly's girl, you said.'

'Maybe she don't go along with that. Whatever, I can hear Herly grindin' his teeth clear back here.'

Seven looked at the slender, shadowy figure in the moonlight fifty feet ahead. 'You think a thing like that'd make him sore at me?'

Hennesey said, 'The surprise wouldn't kill me.'

Before dawn they stopped to water their horses at a creek, and Herly rode over to where Seven and Hennesey had stepped down beside their horses to stretch.

'What do you say, Sergeant?' the lieutenant asked. 'You

10

still figure timing is right to pick them up at Cat Tail?'

Hennesey glanced at the stars above. 'About right, Lieutenant. Nobody knows what a Comanche is goin' to do until he does it. Chances are he don't even know himself. But if they ain't scared we're headin' them off, and if nobody in the bunch is sick or hurt, they'd've hit Cat Tail t'night, and be layin' over.'

Herly pulled sharply on the reins in his hand and his horse brought its head up quickly from water. 'You, Smith, seem to be something of a ladies' man.'

'No, sir, not me.'

Seven could see that Hennesey was grinning faintly.

The sergeant said, 'Truth is, Lieutenant, Smith tells me he joined the Rangers just to be shed of all them pesterin' girls down in Austin.'

Herly spurred his horse over the stream and the other men fell in line behind him.

Seven whispered to Hennesey, 'You tryin' to get me my head blown off?'

'Nope, Sometimes there's a thing to be said that I just can't resist sayin'.' The sergeant settled down into his comfortable position again and said nothing more during their ride.

When they breasted a hill that slanted down fifty feet before them to a wide flat, the stars had disappeared, and Seven could make out a marshy growth of cattails below them that extended along one edge of the flat.

Herly walked his horse to Hennesey. 'We'll wait here, Sergeant. You go out there and take a look around.'

Hennesey handed his reins to Seven. He drew the lever-action Winchester out of its saddle holster and was on the ground in one silent, fluid action. 'I'd advise you t' get back down the hill out of sight till I'm back, Lieutenant.'

He moved down the slope and disappeared soundlessly along the rim of the cattails, and the others rode down off the crest, Seven leading the sergeant's horse.

'If the hostiles are there,' Herly told the men in a soft voice, 'I'll expect to write a good report to headquarters

11

about our dealing with them. Any man who causes me to write something negative will regret it.'

Five minutes went by in a silence so deep Seven could hear his own breathing, and could feel his heart pounding heavily. There was a movement near him and he whirled to find Hennesey standing slightly behind him and to his side.

'Easy, boy. Come for my horse.'

'What did you find?' Herly demanded in a brittle whisper.

'They're in the gully. There is two young bucks who are maybe somewhat dangerous. There's an old man and two kids. They got three horses between 'em. They killed the hog. And they're gettin' up right now, fixin' to drive the two beefs with 'em.'

Herly ran up toward the top of the hill, crouched low. In a moment he was back. 'They're already out on the flat. Mount up.'

Riding to the crest of the hill, Herly spurred into a full gallop and the others thundered over at his side. Seven saw that the small Indian party was only two or three hundred yards away, headed into a growth of three- and four-foot-high cattails. Three Indians mounted. Two boys were on foot behind them, herding the two cows with sticks. The foremost Indian whirled his pony, shouting something to the others, then rode deliberately to the side from which the Rangers would attack, drawing a rifle from a long beaded buckskin holster that ran under his right leg.

The other two mounted Indians started away, changed their minds and reined over beside the leader. One of them had a single-barreled shotgun and the other fitted an arrow to a bow.

'Fire!' Herly yelled, leveling a six-gun at the Comanches and shooting as he gave the order. In the first roar of guns, the old Indian with the shotgun went down. He was spun around sideways on his horse and the shotgun went off as he started to fall, the charge digging up dirt near his horse's hooves. The two younger warriors were riding in swift, plunging, broken lines that made them almost impossible to

12

hit, directing their mounts with leg pressure alone and leaving their arms free for fighting.

While the onrushing Rangers were still a good distance away, the Comanche leader began shooting. He took two shots with the rifle before a Ranger bullet crashed into his shoulder and knocked the gun from his arms. Instantly, two more slugs hit him and he toppled off his pony. The brave with the bow and arrow had plunged straight toward the white men and, since they'd been more concerned with the other Comanche, he was now only forty yards away and the distance was narrowing fast.

Seven was directly in the brave's path. He fired twice, missing both shots and the Comanche let go with an arrow. Seven was vaguely aware that he'd been hit in the leg, and he tried two more shots as the brave sped toward him. The warrior suddenly turned his bow around in his hand and jabbed it at Seven as they rushed together. Seven swung out from his saddle and the bow missed him. Instinctively, Seven slammed his Colt into the brave's face and felt bone crunching as the steel barrel cracked against the warrior's head with a fierce impact gained by two speeding horses. The Comanche was almost dismounted. He'd gone only a few feet beyond Seven when Hennesey shot him in the chest.

'I'd've shot 'im before,' the sergeant said when they pulled their mounts up, 'but you was in the way. That's a fast horse you got.' He glanced at Seven's saddle. 'You come damned close to gettin' a sliver in you there.'

Seven had forgotten the arrow. It was sticking in his saddle so close to his leg that it had ripped his pants. He pulled it out with a shaking hand. 'Looks like it run lengthwise into the leather and didn't hurt my roan.'

Hennesey nodded. 'By the way, thanks for clobberin' that fella with your gun. Otherwise, he'd've had one good chance of killin' me deader'n I care to be.'

Seven's hand was still shaking slightly. 'He didn't have a chance at you,' he said. 'There wasn't time for him to string another arrow.'

Hennesey swung down and went to where the fallen Indian was. He took the long bow from the Comanche's hand and brought it back with him. 'He was too late to stick you. But he'd switched holds in time to get me proper if he'd passed you in one piece.'

Seven took the bow in his hands. One end of the five foot-long weapon had a sharp steel point that made the bow also a deadly lance.

Herly rode up and said, 'What happened to those two children?'

'These fellas put up that scrap so the kids could get away in the cattails,' Hennesey said. 'Reckon we can round 'em up with a little lookin'.'

The lieutenant turned to Seven. 'I've seen some men who can't handle a gun, but you've got them all to beat. That was the worst shooting I've ever witnessed. You had four clear shots at that hostile and missed every time.'

'He was the only one of us who touched a livin' enemy,' Hennesey said mildly. 'Indians consider that the biggest honor of all.'

Herly called to the other men. 'Carson, Priest. Round up the two head of cattle and the Indian ponies. The rest of you come help us look for those kids.'

The Rangers began to ride through the cattails to flush out the Indian children. They'd been at it fifteen minutes and the sun was starting to show in the east when Daggett yelled, 'There they go!'

The two Comanche boys were racing from the edge of the cattails toward the top of a fifteen-foot slope, running with the long, swift strides of a young deer. Herly's revolver roared twice, and the boys were hit. The first one rolled shapelessly back down the hill. The second was bone hit and thrown forceably on over the ridge, arms outspread, by the slamming lead.

Seven sat motionless on his roan, fighting down a hollow sickness that gripped his chest. Hennesey was the only Ranger who moved. He pushed his horse quickly through the marsh and dropped off near the first boy. Then he hurried on foot over the slanting hill to the second. The others rode forward as he returned to his horse near the first youngster.

'The kids are both dead.' He looked down at the boy near his feet. The youngster's back was twisted awkwardly and his eyes were half-open. Thin lines of blood came from one corner of his lips and his nostrils. 'I'd put him about eight years old.' He added flatly, 'There was no call to shoot 'em, Herly.'

Herly flared, 'Five Comanches were stealing cattle! There is nothing that says anything about the age of hostile Comanches!'

## CHAPTER TWO

Herly sent Priest to the Hatcher farm with the livestock, and the rest of the rangers started back toward camp. They made one meal of jerky and bannock, and passed by way of Harrington's Trading Post shortly after dark.

'I'm short on a couple of things,' Herly said. 'You other fellas can come on in. Smith. You stay and keep an eye on the horses.'

Hennesey said, 'Anythin' I can buy for you, Seven?'

'Yeah. Some cigars.'

Seven got down from his roan and leaned idly against the hitching rail where the animals were tied. His legs, stomach and arms were exhausted from nearly forty hours straight in the saddle, and his neck ached. He was rubbing the back of it with one hand when a soft feminine voice spoke pleasantly behind him. 'Stiff neck?'

He turned and Joy was standing there, the light from the windows making her blonde hair glow faintly at the edges. 'Yes, ma'am – miss. Stiff as frozen rawhide.'

'Call me Joy. Sergeant Hennesey said you wanted some cigars. I wanted a breath of fresh air, so I brought them out to you.' She handed him a small, round bundle of thin black cigars bound with a piece of twine. 'These are the best we have. They're fifty cents to the dozen.'

Seven reached into his pocket, but she said, 'Oh, that's all right. The men in Company D usually pay us when they get paid, at the end of the month. Sergeant Hennesey says you saved his life.' She leaned against the hitching rail near Seven as he unwrapped the cigars and put them evenly in his jacket and shirt pockets.

'He told me that, too. Though truth to tell, it was mostly by accident.'

'Will you be at the Caldwell barn-raising next week?'

'I didn't know about it – don't know if the lieutenant is much for lettin' the men off for things like that – or what.' He added hesitantly, 'Especially, Miss Joy, since, well – I got the feelin' he ain't too fond of me.'

She smiled. 'Is he fond of anyone?'

'No, I guess not, aside from yourself.'

'Me?' Her smile moved into soft laughter. 'Oh, I suppose he likes me in his way.'

'In his way?' Seven pushed his hat back in mild surprise. 'But I was told that you and him, had a sort of an understandin'.'

She shook her head. 'Not at all.'

'Well, if I can get to the Caldwell's barn-raisin', I sure will be there.'

'There will be dancing and things, after the roof's up. I'll save you a dance.'

'I'm most flattered that you would do that. I expect a dance with you carries a high value.'

Harrington come onto the gallery with a lantern. The Rangers came behind him and Joy said, 'It's nice to have you brave men staying so close.' Her words were half in fun and half true. 'It's a good feeling when the Comanches are around.'

Dagget laughed and said, 'You can bet your bottom dollar Harrington's is the first place we'd protect, Miss Joy. Got the prettiest girl and the best whiskey in West Texas.'

Herly came down off the gallery and paused before Joy. 'Will you be at the Caldwell's next Thursday?'

'Yes. We were just talking about that.'

Herly glanced at Smith with narrowing eyes. 'Then I'll hope to have the pleasure of seeing you there, Miss Joy. And of having a dance with you.'

'Why of course, Lieutenant.'

On the way to their camp along the Devil, Seven gave Hennessey a cigar and took one himself. When the smokes were lighted, Hennesey said, 'I was never any good at tellin' whether a man was a handsome dog or not, but you must be, Seven.'

'She ain't got no understandin' with Herly. She said so.'

'No?'

'She'd sure be a nice girl to have for a girl.' Smith coughed slightly over his cigar and Hennesey said, 'These black Mexican stogies are hellish at first, but they're a mighty fine smoke when you get 'em mastered.'

A corporal named Warren who had been down along the border was in camp when the Rangers returned. Seven was cooking a frying pan full of beans for supper when Warren and Hennesey squatted around the fire near him. The sergeant put a small metal grill over the fire and balanced a pot of coffee on it. He said to Warren, 'Heard ya' talkin' to Herly about Flood. Got any late news on on that hell-roarin' character?'

'He's headed back for Texas, seems like. Bank was robbed in Socorro. Three fellas kilt, another damned near dead, accordin' to the telegraph down in Del Rio. There was just the one man, and he robbed the bank by his lonesome and had the whole town half scared to death. That's Flood.'

'What about this here Flood?' Seven asked Hennesey.

'You ain't heard of 'im?'

'Well, yeah, but kind of in the same way a fella hears of Sam Bass or Wild Bill Hickok. You don't hardly know nothin' about 'em exceptin' a few wild, exaggerated stories.'

'Any exaggerated story you ever heard about Flood, just

multiply it by nine hundred,' Hennesey said, 'and you got a true picture of 'im.'

'What's he comin' back to Texas for?' Seven took the beans away from the fire and stirred them with a spoon so they wouldn't burn on the bottom.

'Partly, I guess, because he's a Texan an' he likes Texas,' Hennesey said.

'And one more little thing,' Warren added dryly. 'He said he'd kill the men who took 'im in last time. Leastwise, he swore he'd kill four of 'em. Four peace officers up to Lubbock. If I was them, I'd be God-awful edgy about now.'

'He said he'd kill four of them?' Seven asked. 'How the hell many did it take?'

'Five,' Hennesey told him. 'And then they wouldn'ta got 'im if he hadn't been dead drunk an' without guns for once. As it was, he damned near killed a couple of 'em when they piled him.'

'Friend Hennesey here,' Warren said, 'was the fifth man in the bunch. How come he didn't say he'd get you, Hennesey?'

'I don't know,' the sergeant shrugged. 'Maybe 'cause we was friends one time. Maybe 'cause I stopped the others from shootin' him when they had 'im down that way. Or, maybe, Jim plain forgot to mention me when he was rantin' around in jail. Never got a chance to talk to 'im afterwards. They extradited him to Arizona right away. Seems he'd killed more fellas out there than anybody ever got around to countin'.'

'How is it they didn't hang 'im?' Seven took the beans from the fire. 'Anybody want any beans?' Neither of them accepted, so Seven sat back and began eating from the frying pan.

'They was goin' to hang Flood for certain,' Warren said. 'Guess that's why he took it in mind to leave.'

'You think he'll be after you, Hennesey?' Seven asked.

'Don't know.' The sergeant took a bandanna from his pocket and grabbed the coffee pot from the fire before the flames could burn him. 'I hope to hell not.'

18

# CHAPTER THREE

During the next week Seven rode to the tiny settlement of Barnstaff Bend with Sergeant Hennesey to check the report that a wanted man was there. After waiting two days with no sign of the fugitive, they made the long ride back to the Devil River camp.

James was chopping firewood as they rode in, and he called to Hennesey. 'Hey, Sergeant. Hoyt just come in from Sonora, couple hours ago. He got it over the wireless there that Flood was up to Lubbock!'

Hennesey whistled. 'That man does travel fast.'

'Was in Lubbock one day. Three of them four fellas who took him was found with various and sundry holes in 'em. Dead.'

Hennesey unsaddled his horse and threw the leather seat over a log. Seven leaned down from where he still sat his roan, listening intently. 'What about the fourth man?'

James wiped his face with the back of his hand. 'It don't seem that nobody knows what happened to him. He just plain disappeared. Maybe Flood ate 'im for breakfast. Maybe he got in a hole and pulled it in after 'im.'

'By God!' Seven said firmly. 'I'd sure hate t' meet that Flood on a dark night!'

James went back to cutting wood. 'Wouldn't be no fun on a sunny day, neither.'

'Let's go check in with Herly,' the sergeant told Seven.

They walked to the lieutenant's tent and Hennesey rapped twice on the tent pole. 'Hennesey and Smith.'

'Come in,' Herly called.

The sergeant pulled open the flap and they entered the tent. Herly was lying on a folding bunk, reading a yellow pamphlet. 'What happened at Barnstaff Bend?'

'Nothin'.'

Herly sat up with his legs over the edge of the bed. 'You

19

two sure wasted a lot of time for nothing.' He shook his head. 'I finally got Captain Gresham to let us take quarters here on a more permanent basis, Sergeant. We'll be renting that big chicken coop Harrington's got out behind his post. Plenty of room. I want you to take James, Hoyt and Carson to Harrington's some time in the morning and start getting the place ready. We ought to be able to move in by Friday.'

When the sun was lowering over the river, Dagget came to where Seven was whittling on a stick. 'Herly says t' see 'im right away in his tent.'

The lieutenant glanced up at Seven's approach and his cold eyes bored into him. 'Everybody here wants to go to the Caldwell barn-raising tonight. Since – you're the newest man here, you got the duty of watching camp.' He stood up and added flatly, 'I think we understand each other, Smith.'

That night Seven sat alone for a long time near the dimly glowing coals of the campfire. He whistled softly, experimenting with a song he'd heard James singing before, 'Pony Boy.' Before turning in, he went to check the livestock once more. The mules were quiet and half asleep. He stroked his roan's neck. 'What do ya think of this miserable damned outfit?' he asked the roan. 'We oughta be out dancin' and drinkin' and havin' a time for ourselves. Instead we're wastin' our life away guardin' a bunch of junk, mules and tents.'

There was the faint sound of horses moving toward the camp. Seven waited where he was, hidden in the shadows near the roan.

The riders appeared darkly out of the gloom and a vaguely familiar voice called, 'Smith! You sleepin'?'

'No, sir. That you, Mister Harrington?'

'Yeah. Where are ya? Oh, there you are. It's me and my crazy daughter,' Harrington complained as Seven walked forward. 'She leaves the party early 'cause of the headache, then decides to ride two miles outta the way so's we can say hello to you. Harrington women-folks've always been diffi- cult.'

20

Joy unhooked her knee from the prone of a sidesaddle and jumped lightly to the ground. 'It wasn't fair. You are the only person in twenty miles that wasn't at the Caldwell's.' She reached into her small black purse that matched the trim, high-necked dress she was wearing under a warm sheepskin-lined coat. 'Ray Caldwell was passing out cigars for his newest born. We took one for you.'

'And I got us somethin' better'n that.' Harrington slapped his coat pocket.

'Well,' Seven said awkwardly, 'it was sure nice of you both to ride out of your way like that.'

Seven added wood to the coals and put a pot of fresh coffee over the flames. He went to Hennesey's tent and got the folding chair for Joy to sit on. 'I guess you can see that it ain't the Rangers that keeps the State of Texas broke,' he apologized. 'Things are about as unfancy as they can get.'

'Here.' Harrington passed his flask to Seven. 'It'll give us somethin' to work on while coffee's heatin'.'

'Well.' Seven took a small drink and swallowed it. 'Thank you, sir. But I'd better not take any more. Seein' I'm s'posed to be lookin' out for the camp here.'

They had coffee and Seven had lighted his cigar when Harrington leaned back against a mule pack ready to be loaded in the morning and said, 'You kids go ahead an' talk. Gimme about thirty, forty minutes to sleep or I'll be dead in the early hours tomorrow.' He pulled his hat down over his eyes and sighed as he relaxed.

Seven smiled across the fire at Joy. 'Maybe I could take you for a walk down by the river?'

'All right.'

They went into the deep shadows beyond the fire and Seven took Joy by the hand to lead her to a log near the water's edge. They sat in silence for a long time, listening to the busy gurgle and wash where the river rolled against the land in tireless rhythm.

Finally Seven said quietly, 'I want you to know that I sure appreciate your stoppin' by this way. I think it's about the nicest thing I ever heard of.'

'Dad and I like you. There's only about one party a year around here. It didn't seem right for you to be alone the whole night.'

'I consider your comin' here this way better than any party I was ever at.' Seven added quickly, 'Miss Joy, I take it that you are not – lettin' any one special man call on you. I mean—'

'No special man,' she said. 'I'm free of ties.'

'I guess you already know, more or less, that Lieutenant Herly is pretty taken by you. And he's a lot more than me. He's an officer, an' all.'

She shook her head faintly. 'I've never been too fond of him.'

'Then if it's all right with you, Miss Joy, I will call on you whenever I can. And – it will be most serious on my part.'

She laughed. 'Well, don't be overly serious. I like the fact that you smile easily. And I'll look forward to receiving you.'

Later, back at the fire, Seven touched Harrington's shoulder and the man mumbled faintly, then opened his eyes.

Joy tilted his hat back on his head. 'Come on, sleepyhead. You've got to be up at five o'clock. And we've still got a ride in front of us.'

Seven helped Joy up to the sidesaddle and her father groaningly hoisted himself aboard his mount.

They had been gone only a few minutes when Seven heard a large group of horses coming up along the river. 'Hello, the camp!' a loud, drunken voice called out. 'Company D reportin' to headquarters!'

'Be it ever so humble,' another echoed, 'which it sure is!'

The men stripped their horses and crowded around the fire as one of them began to stir it up. Hennesey took his saddle into his tent and came out to where Seven was standing near the others. 'How'd it go?'

'Fine. The Harringtons stopped by on their way home.'

'Well how d'ya like that!' someone grumbled loudly, hearing Seven's remark. 'If you can't come to the party, the goddamned party comes to you! Your luck just ain't believeable!'

Herly, on his way to his tent, cut over toward them. 'What's that talk about parties here?'

'Not a party exactly,' Seven said. 'I was just sayin' the Harringtons came by the camp on their way home.'

'So what happened?' Herly asked in a voice that was almost a whisper.

'Nothin' much. They was simply nice enough to bring me a cigar and a drink.'

'You drank here on duty?'

'I took a taste to be sociable.'

Herly's hand whipped out viciously and he slapped Seven so hard the crack of sound made everyone in camp turn to face them. 'That's for drinking on duty.' He brought his hand back swiftly and lashed Seven with his knuckles. 'And that's for not addressing me as sir!'

Seven stepped back, slightly unbalanced by the blows. Herly whirled instantly and went into his tent in a few long strides, jerking the flap down behind him.

Seven's face was tight with stinging pain and fury. He took two steps toward Herly's tent and found Hennesey suddenly barring the way. The sergeant said, 'No.'

'Hell,' Carson sneered in a low voice, 'I know what I'd do if somebody tried to slap me.'

'That's interestin',' Hennesey said. 'I always admire you uncommon tough men.' He suddenly backhanded Carson. 'Show me what you'd do.'

Carson was dumbfounded. His rage showed for a brief moment and then he decided to make a joke of it. 'I'd slug some bastard that didn't outrank me!' He shoved James, who was standing near him, and the two men wrestled drunkenly before someone tripped them and they fell heavily to the ground, goaded on in their friendly fight by yells and laughter.

Hennesey turned back to Seven. 'If a man pulls a knife or gun, you take steps. Otherwise, no. Insults was invented

23

to help little people feel big. A good man don't bother with
'em one way or the other.'

Seven nodded. 'Maybe. What would you've done if he hit
you?'

'Probably about what you was startin' to do. But I'd
hope to have a fella around who'd stop me from makin' an
ass of myself.'

## CHAPTER FOUR

Company D was mounted and moving away from the Devil
half an hour after breakfast. The column of twelve horse-
men and nine pack mules wound through the hills and flats
to the northeast and arrived at Harrington's while the morning sun was still low in the east. The chicken coop which was
to be their new headquarters was a long, low, stout frame
building a hundred yards behind the Trading Post.

One end of the building had been walled off to make an
office, and a door that had not yet been fitted to the frame
was leaning against the wall.

'The far end there,' Hennesy told them, 'will be a cell. We
get the middle twenty-five feet of space. We'll build in bunks
directly. Time bein', just spread your bedrolls on the softest
places you can find on the floor.'

That afternoon a corporal from Company C rode through
and stopped off to talk to Herly in his office.

Seven was currying his horse where the Rangers' animals
were stabled in Harrington's barn when Joy came into the
barn and said, 'Hello, there. The men like their new place?'

'Yes, it's fine.' Seven could see that Joy was angry. She
was wearing a shirt and britches, and she climbed into the
loft to fork down hay for her father's five horses.

'Somethin' got you upset, Miss Joy?'

She paused in her work. 'Yes. Herley. He seems to think
he's taking over the whole Trading Post. And he called Dad
down for giving you a drink last night. So I told him what

24

I thought of him.' She went back to throwing wispy cascades of hay into the mangers below.' He said he'd see that none of the boys bothered us, and I told him I'd given you permission to visit us any time you wanted and I thought he was actually going to explode.'

Seven leaned over his roan's back and grinned up at her. 'I would say my future in the Rangers at this minute ain't too bright.'

She jabbed the pitchfork into a mound of hay and climbed down from the loft. Leaning on the other side of the quietly munching roan, she said, 'We Harrington women have never put up with nonsense. For the first time today, I realized that Walter Herly thinks he has a hold on me. And he has no right. You are welcome – invited – to see us when you choose. And if he doesn't like it, he can go chase himself!'

James came into the barn and tipped his hat to Joy. 'Afternoon, Miss Harrington. Seven, Herly wants to see you and Hennesey right away. You seen the sergeant?'

'No.'

'You go ahead. I'll hunt 'im up.' James smiled at Joy and went out the other side of the big barn.

Joy's anger turned to worry and she said, 'I hope I won't be the cause of the trouble. But the things I've said here are true.' Her hand was resting on the roan's back, and Seven put his own hand over hers with gentle pressure. 'Any trouble you might cause would be worthwhile trouble,' he smiled.

Lieutenant Herly was sitting behind a small table he was using as a desk. He looked at Seven, his dark, half-closed eyes hiding whatever feelings were behind them. 'Come in, Smith. No point in saying what I've got to say twice. Sit down and wait till Hennesey gets here.'

Seven sat on a bench that had been placed along one wall of the office. Two long, deadly silent minutes went slowly by before Hennesey entered the room and Herly waved him to a chair near the desk.

'Corporal Kline was here on his way to Fort Davis,' the lieutenant said. 'He brought an interesting bit of news with him. James Flood was seen at a point this side of Sanderson, headed toward the Stockton Plateau. That puts him close enough to Company D, I believe, to warrant action on our part. I've decided to take a strong stand in regard to Flood.'

'A strong stand?' Hennesey asked.

Herly glanced at Seven. 'I've decided to send you two out to get Flood.'

Hennesey stared thoughtfully out of a window behind Herly. 'That's a big order.'

'Two men against one man?'

'That ain't two men against one man. That's two men against Jim Flood. Less'n six men trailin' him are just askin' for a one-way ticket to glory.'

'Sergeant Hennesey, are you afraid of the duty I'm assigning you?'

Hennesey stood up. 'When do we leave?'

'As soon as you can get saddles on your horses.' Herly got up from his chair. 'Another thing. This won't be a simple check on the Stockton Plateau, or a routine investigation. This will be a manhunt. I want Flood, and I want Company D to get him. Follow him to China if you have to, but get him and bring him back. I want him jailed at the other end of this building while Lubbock and Austin and El Paso and the other towns wrangle over who gets the honor of hanging him.'

'You ain't insistin' we try an' take 'im alive, necessarily?'

Herly shook his head. 'No. I can't do that. But I want him alive if possible.'

'I'd rather have Hoyt go with me than Smith.'

'Why?'

'Hoyt's a first class Ranger an' gunman. Smith ain't.' Hennesey's voice became gruff. 'You know damn well, Lieutenant, that Flood is a pure, straight-grain demon in any kind of a fight. He could shoot Smith six times afore the boy had time t' bat an eyelash.'

'Smith joined the Rangers. That's the chance he has to take.'

'We'll be gone inside of ten minutes,' Hennesey said. 'But

there's a thing you oughta know now. There ain't nobody who won't know your real interest. I'll say no more.'

Hennesey turned and went out of the door. Seven got up and walked past the tight-lipped lieutenant to follow the sergeant.

Herly called in a hard, low voice, 'Smith.'

Seven turned back, waiting for him to continue.

'You don't have to go. This isn't the army. You can admit you're scared and get out of the Rangers.' He paused. 'Although cowardice wouldn't look too good to – say the Harringtons, for example.'

'Truth is,' Seven told him, 'I ain't at all scared. I ain't never seen a man I admired so much as Sergeant Hennesey. We'll wrap a pink ribbon around Flood and bring 'im back as a present for you. —Sir.'

Herly grinned very faintly. 'You think so, Smith?'

As the news of their assignment spread, Seven noticed a growing stillness in the Ranger station. He was rolling up his blanket when Hennesey walked by with his saddle over his shoulder. 'I'll bring your roan down, Seven. See you outside.'

'Thanks.'

James wandered over and sat on his heels near Seven. 'You and the sergeant're goin' off after Flood, huh?'

'That's right.' Seven tied the roll and put it under his arm.

'Well.' James rubbed his moustache with the back of his hand. 'Luck, boy.' He stood up and went back to lie down on his bed.

Seven went outside where Hennesey was bringing the horses up. While they were saddling the animals, several of the other men wandered out to gather in a half circle around them.

Hoyt said, 'I hear Flood always keeps a spare six-gun on him some place. Might be well to bear in mind.'

Seven pulled himself up into the saddle and settled the Winchester holstered under his leg more comfortably. Hennesey was already mounted.

'Good luck huntin' that wolf,' Warren said.

27

'So long, boys.' Hennesey reined his bay around and he and Seven rode away from the station.

Seven said, 'Never seen them carry on so. You'd think we was on the way to a funeral.'

Hennesey glanced at the trading post. 'Harrington's daughter is out on the front gallery. You wanna ride over and tell 'er adios?'

'Yeah.' Seven squeezed his roan into a jog and pulled the mare up by the gallery. 'Hennesey and me are goin' to go try to find a fella,' he told her.

'Think you'll be gone long?' Joy balanced the big bottle of vinegar she'd picked up on the gallery railing and brushed a curl of blonde hair back from her eyes.

'Hard to say. But I'll sure be lookin' forward to comin' back here.'

She smiled at him. 'And I'll be waiting for you to call.'

Seven rejoined Hennesey and they had soon left the buildings out of sight behind them.

'You think,' Seven finally said, 'that we'll have our hands full gettin' Flood back?'

'I think so. You got any cigars?'

There were a few in Seven's saddlebags and he got two of them out. When they lighted their smokes, Hennesey said, 'At the very least, we're goin' to have ourselves a merry chase. That man gets around like three Pony Express riders. There's two things, also, I'd like for you t'remember.' He blew cigar smoke out to near his horse's ears where it began to rise and vanish in the air. 'If anythin' should happen to me, you are to get the hell back to the station. Second, under absolutely no conditions whatever are you to try to take Flood alone.'

'Well, Hennesey, there's situations and situations.'

'I'll be honest with you, Seven. In any situation, for you to try to take Flood alone would be like tryin' to douse a forest fire with a spoonful of water.' Hennesey turned toward Seven and said, 'Now I tol' you not to get insulted, if possible. It's a waste of energy. Jus' face the facts. Flood is a

28

goddamned tornado in a fight. He ain't the one for a young and inexperienced fella to cut his teeth on.'

Seven said nothing.

'Unload one of them Colts,' Hennesey told him.

'What?'

'Unload one o' your guns.'

As Seven began removing cartridges, Hennesey said, 'I want you to spend lots of time in the saddle simply foolin' with that gun. Pullin' it. Puttin' it back. Twirlin' it on your finger. Anythin' that comes to mind to do with it. I want you to know by weight alone whether it's loaded or not. I want it to get to be as much a part of your whole arm as your hand is. And from time to time we'll practise shootin', see if we got the makin's of a gunfighter in you.'


## CHAPTER FIVE

After three days, when the two men had crossed the Pecos River and were close to the town of Sanderson, they came to a wooden shack huddled for protection from the north wind under a fifteen-foot cutback cliff.

'Sheepherder,' Hennesey decided. He called out, 'Anybody home?'

The flimsy door creaked open and a little old woman peered blinkingly out at them.

'You hear tell, lately, of a man around here named Jim Flood?'

The old woman came out of the door and stood on the second of two rickety steps leading up from the ground. 'Why sure, mister. He was here not more'n a week ago or so. He had beans and coffee with my man and me.' She stopped with sudden suspicion. 'And what might you be wantin' with 'im?'

'Just tryin' to find 'im is all. Are you real sure it was Flood who was here, ma'am?'

'Sure?' The woman's voice sang with resentment and she

fumbled in the pocket of her faded blue apron. 'Lookit here, mister! A ten dollar gold piece!' She raised the gleaming coin. 'No common saddlebum never gave no poor, hard-workin' old woman a present like that for coffee and beans. It was that fine Mister Flood, never doubt. He was just passin' on his way up north.'

'What kind of horse was he ridin' ma'am?'

'A big handsome paint. I tell you— he cut the finest figure of a man!'

Hennesey nodded. 'Flood's partial to paints.' He asked the woman, 'Never said any special place up north he was headin'?'

'No. Say, who are you fellas, anyhow?'

'Rangers.'

'Rangers? Well you won't get nothin' outta me! Pesterin' a body half t' death with fool questions!' She went back in and slammed the door.

Hennesey pointed his bay north. 'Let's go, boy.'

Seven turned back for one last look at the shack and saw the old woman peering out after them through a cracked window. 'She sure didn't care for the Rangers.'

'They like ya' best when they're in trouble.'

'She seemed to've liked Flood.'

'Everybody does. 'Till he kills 'em.'

They rode for days that turned slowly into weeks, asking questions as they went, sleeping mostly under the open sky, sometimes beddding down in small-town hotels or a friendly farmer's loft. It seemed that Flood had been everywhere they passed, or near enough that the people could say something of him. He had ridden through a week ago, ten days ago, two weeks ago. He'd never stayed long, and everywhere he'd passed, he'd made friends. People bragged of the chair in their parlor he'd sat on, they spoke warmly of the things he'd said, and they kept the ten-dollar gold pieces he was passing out generously – kept them as mementos of the famous outlaw's visit, rather than spend them.

The two men went far into the Stockton Plateau, then replaced their direction with a west-northwest trail where

Flood had headed back toward the Pecos at right angles. They trailed him through half a dozen settlements and small towns, finally moving north once more. At Odessa Hennesey said, 'I'm broke flat. We better send a telegraph wire to Austin and see if we can get 'em to come across with a few dollars travelin' money. We'll lay over in this town till tomorrow.'

That night they went into the Red River Saloon for a drink. It was a big, noisy place, and they took their drinks to a table in the quietest corner of the room.

'We been gone over a month now,' Seven said. 'It sure is takin' us a long time t' locate that fella.'

Hennesey nodded. 'Maybe Flood found out that the terrible Seven Ways From Sundown Smith was on his trail and is reformed. I never knew him to go so damned long with no trouble.'

'Well, what I mean, hell, we could spend the rest of our lives lookin' for 'im.' Seven drank his whiskey and sighed. 'How long do ya' go on?'

'Seems t' me some fella back a while ago spent more'n two years chasin' down a fugitive. And that Ranger went all through Mexico and once into Canada. That gunman he was after finally died, though whether from the Ranger's bullets or old age. I don't rightly know.'

A young, dark-eyed girl with long brown hair came to the table and said, 'Buy me a drink?'

Hennesey looked up at her, taking in the flashy, low-cut dress. 'Sorry, lady.'

The girl sat down anyway and said, 'Please. I'll buy my own drink if you want. But I have to talk to you.'

Hennesey said, 'What about?'

A barman in a greasy apron appeared and the girl said, 'The same, Charlie.' When he'd gone, she leaned forward. 'They say you're looking for Jim Flood.'

'Who says?'

'People who know these things.' She hesitated. 'You, you are not lawmen?'

31

Hennesey shook his head in disgust. 'Don't see no badges on us, do ya?'

The barman brought her drink and Hennesey paid for it. She reached her closed fist toward him, palm down, to give him the money for her drink, and he pushed her hand away gently. 'What's your interest in Flood?'

'Very simple. I was with him two nights ago. When you find him, I want you to tell him that Lucinda loves him and will marry him any time he wants.'

Hennesey shifted in his chair uncomfortably. 'I'd be pleased to relay that message, but I'm havin' one hard time findin' old Jim.'

She stood up. 'He left heading north. Please tell him what I said.' She clasped her hands together for a moment. 'He'll know all the other things I'd like to tell him.'

When she'd left the table, Seven said, 'That must be the third or fourth girl he's left behind already. 'Pears to me if we banded all them unhappy females together, they'd have 'im found in no time. There'd be a whole damn batallion.'

'He's handy with everythin'. Women, horses, guns, fists – even words. I swear he could talk a preacher into burnin' his Bible.'

Hennesey got the money he'd wired for the next day, and they rode on to the north, at last reaching the Mustang river. Here, it seemed, Flood had followed the river upstream, heading toward New Mexico.

'He's hittin' into the Staked Plains country,' Hennesey said.' Maybe he's goin' back to that bank he robbed, to rob it again. Or to apologize. You can never say jus' what Flood is agoin' to do next.'

They were well into the Staked Plain and had made a dry camp the night before when Seven was awakened by a rough shake of his shoulder. 'Get up,' Hennesey told him.

'Okay,' Seven yawned. 'Ain't it a little early? Not even light yet.' He stopped talking and came wide awake as he saw a great, red glow suffusing the dark sky to the west. 'Fire?'

'Pretty big one.' Hennesey pushed a bit into his horse's mouth. 'We better go have a look.'

They rode three miles through the tall grass that was waving gently in the morning breeze. It slowly became lighter as sunrise approached, and when they crested a low hill they could see everything clearly in the wide, sandy basin that lay before them. Half a mile away a barn and house were still burning brightly at the edge of a small town. Perhaps a hundred people were formed into two bucket-chains stretching out to nearby wells, but they had no chance of saving the house. They weren't even bothering with the barn.

The two men rode down into the basin. A few hundred feet from the blazing buildings, Hennesey suddenly stopped his horse, and following the sergeant's gaze, Seven saw a man lying face down on the ground. The back of the man's head had been sheared off as though he'd been hit with a hard-swinging axe.

'Nothin' nobody can do for him,' Hennesey muttered. They went on to the town and dismounted at the edge of the crowd still gathering around the fire. 'What happened?' Seven asked a young man with smoke-blackened hair and face, who was leaning exhaustedly over a handcart.

Breathing heavily, the young man said, 'Don't rightly know. Oney one thing certain is a man named Jim Flood got riled at this town.'

'You got a mayor, or a town council or somethin'?' Hennesey asked him.

'Nope. Closest we got is Horace Brush, in the white hat over there. He owns the hardware and dry goods store.'

A fat man in a white Steson was standing in a small circle of men near a shed closer into town. Hennesey led his bay toward the group and Seven followed, noticing a man on the other side of the burning house as he walked. The man was stretched out on a blanket, naked to the waist. The chest was wrapped in a big bandage and two women were kneeling beside him, caring for him.

Hennesey stopped near the fat man who had wide cheeks,

33

a tight mouth, and small, suspicious eyes. 'Mister Brush? Understand you are the closest thing to mayor around here. Like t' find out what happened.'

'Who are you?' Brush demanded curtly.

'We're lawmen. Lookin' for Jim Flood.'

'Why didn't you get here yesterday? You're too late now!'

'Can you say with any accuracy what happened, and which way Flood headed?'

'You bet I can tell you what happened, fella! Flood got here yesterday mornin'. First off, he left his horse at Fenton's Hostelry.' Brush raised his voice as one of the walls of the big barn caved in with a crushing roar that sent armies of sparks whirling high into the air. 'That barn was the hostelry. He wanted his pony shod. Later in the day he come to my place, wantin' to buy matches an' a new shirt. I sold 'em to him and he said, real pleasant and friendly. 'A little high, wouldn't you say?' So I told 'im that might be, but we set our own prices out here, and folks don't like the prices, they can go to the nearest competition which is eighty miles away. I didn't know who he was, or I'd've made him a deal. Last evenin' he went to see his horse and Fenton told 'im the shoein' would run nine dollars.'

'Hell,' Seven said, 'three's a good price.'

'What we charge is our business, and nobody else's,' Brush said. 'Anyhow, last night he got in a poker game with some of the boys and started losin' pretty heavy. That's the last I knew till I got back at around three o'clock this mornin'. Had to ride out of town to collect an overdue payment from a chiselin' family out by Dead Dog Point.'

'It was 'bout midnight when Flood blew up,' a short, bald man at Brush's side told them. 'There was him and four others aplayin' stud over at Hansel's place. He killed two of 'em in Hansel's and the third one we found over there.' The man pointed toward the bandaged man lying on the ground. 'He's lung shot. Doubt he'll last. Fourth man ain't showed up.'

Hennesey nodded back in the direction from which they'd

approached the town. 'Reckon you'll find 'im out there in a clump of grass. No hurry about pickin' him up.'

Brush shook his head. 'It's sure a pity what he did to this town. I couldn't feel more poorly about the sufferin' of these poor citizens.' He scratched his nose. 'But it's done, and there ain't no use cryin' about it now, I guess.'

'Did anyone see him leave town?' Hennesey asked.

The first thing they felt was an immense shock wave, as though an invisible force was trying to throw them to the ground, and hard after it came a booming roar of sound that pounded at their ears with almost physical force. An instant later the thunderous explosion was echoing far out on the hills. Seven picked up his hat that had been knocked off, before he realized his roan had broken away behind him and was galloping out onto the flat in panic. The man next to Brush had been sent sprawling by the shockwave. The people fighting the fire stood stunned, in motionless indecision.

And then odds and ends of things began falling. A ten-foot-long plank walloped the ground a few feet from where Hennesey stood gripping the reins of his rearing horse. A section of shingled roof landed on the shed behind Brush, and a long piece of rope snaked down out of the sky to the ground near one chain of volunteer fire-fighters.

After a moment of frozen silence, a man came running around a nearby building and shouted, 'Horace! It's your place!'

'What?' Brush screamed.

'Even the places alongside you are all caved in! You better come look!'

The people started to leave the hopeless fire and investigate the explosion, and Seven took off toward the flat on a run to get his roan. The mare stopped two hundred yards out and looked back with trembling distrust. 'C'mon,' Seven called. 'It's okay. Get back here.' He whistled low between his teeth. 'Don't go female on me now.'

She finally settled down enough that he could walk up

to her, and he soothed her a moment before mounting and riding back to the town.

Most of the windows on the small main street were shattered, and several doors were off their hinges. The crowd had gathered around what had been, evidently, a large building. Now it was a crumpled, broken mass of debris, and the empty space it had filled before looked like a missing tooth in a broad smile. The barber shop on one side and the saloon on the other had been damaged badly. Each of their adjacent walls were caved in and raggedly warped and splintered.

Hennesey was holding his bay away from the crowd and Seven rode over to him. 'What happened?'

'One of Flood's little gestures of esteem, looks like. Brush had a couple cases of dynamite and two, three hundred yards of slow-burnin' fuse in 'is store. Jus' lucky nobody was killed. It made quite a pop.'

Brush strode over to where the two men were, his face pale with fury. His fat cheeks shaking with rage, he said, 'What're you lawmen goin' to do about my store? I'm wiped out! Everythin' gone while you sit here and do nothin'!'

'It's done,' Hennesey said. 'No use cryin' about it now.' He mounted his bay. 'Anyone see 'im leave town?'

A big, slow-spoken man who'd come up behind Brush said, 'He went due west. I saw him ride out.'

'Obliged, mister.' Hennesey pushed his bay into a trot down the street and, with Seven beside him, moved into a lope once out of town.

The sun was now warm on the back of Seven's neck. He said, 'Think we'll catch up to 'im today?'

'Maybe.'

'He must've been crazy mad to wreck that town that way.'

'Flood is never crazy mad. He jus' gets irritated sometimes. Save your breath. We got a ride ahead.'

It was then that Seven noticed for the first time that Hennesey was following a horse's tracks in the sandy ground.

36

They were the only fresh tracks moving west over the floor of the broad basin. The sergeant only glanced at the hoof-prints ahead once in a while to assure himself of direction. Most of the time his eyes were scanning the low hills that lay ahead.

## CHAPTER SIX

They got to the top of a high hill in the late afternoon and a vast, rolling plane stretched out for miles before them. Hennesey said quietly, 'Look.'

Seven glanced at the sergeant to see where his eyes were set. Then he stared against the sun at that part of the western horizon. On a far away hill he thought he saw a movement. He squinted his eyes and saw, briefly, the faint suggestion of a tiny, dark speck that moved over the crest of the hill and disappeared. 'Him?'

'Uh, huh,' Hennesey grunted.

'How far off is he?'

'Five, six miles.'

'Chase 'im down?'

'Kill the horses. They already done near forty miles at a pretty fair clip.'

'What's he ridin'? A damned machine?'

'Never knew of Flood ridin' a horse worth under two hundred dollars. All we can do is hope he slows down.'

They went down the slope before them at a walk.

Early the next morning they hit a wide flat full of shale and rock, and Flood's trail was lost.

'Have to circle this whole damned thing,' Hennesey said, 'to pick up his sign again.'

'I could go one way and you t'other.'

'We'll stick together.'

They lost two hours winding around the flat. By the time they located the place where Flood had left the flat Hennesey began frowning at the sky. 'Hardly ever rains 'round here,' he muttered. 'Be just our luck.'

Dark clouds gathered low to the north and edged slowly into the sky above them, shoving back the clear blue as they came on relentlessly.

Hennesey pulled his bay to a halt. 'Better git out your slicker, boy.'

The rain came in a sudden rush, hard-hitting and cold, and they rode on into the growing sea of mud. An hour later, with the rain still pounding down from above, they climbed a ridge and there was a wide river winding down the middle of the valley stretching out before them. The sergeant tilted his head carefully, to spill the rain from his hat without letting raindrops get down his neck. 'The Pecos again. And there sure ain't no trail left to folla'.'

'What'll we do?'

'Don't know. Can't see him doublin' back t'ward the Loco Hills, or goin' up toward ol' Fort Sumner. An' I can't see 'im pushin' his horse across river here. Pecos is movin' kinda fast down there, and he'd likely get his horse banged up.' Hennesey shrugged. 'Let's go down stream some.'

At Lake McMillan that night, they talked to a prospector who was living in a ragged tent near the north end of the lake.

'Yessir,' the man said positively. 'Seen that very man you're talkin' about. Big pinto pony he was on. He let his pony rest a bit, passin' by here. He got off an' went down by the shore and was throwin' rocks out into the water. He must've tossed a hundred rocks – skippin' 'em across the top some a' the time, like a li'l boy'll do for fun.'

'You didn't talk to 'im?' Hennesey said.

'Nope. After a while he went on south along the lake.'

Hennesey thanked the prospector, and they rode on as the sergeant muttered, 'Tossin' rocks in the water – while it was rainin', too. Just like a little kid.'

Riding along the lake, Hennesey said, 'That there is Flood all right. That man could've been anything he wanted to be in this world, if he'd growed up. But he'd rather stay a big kid. Throwin' pebbles in the lake, raisin' unholy hell . . .' His voice trailed off thoughtfully.

Seven and Hennesey found the days growing into weeks once more as they pushed on after their man. They were within a few minutes of seeing him at Dark Canyon, farther south, according to a rancher they met who was out rounding up a stray calf. Then Seven's roan went lame and wouldn't walk. Seven found a cactus needle buried deep in the mare's fetlock and he got it out, but she limped for two days and he spent most of the time walking beside her.

They rode on across New Mexico, riding over the Guadalupe Mountains and eventually coming down off the Organ Range into Las Cruces. Ten days later, with Flood somewhere between four days and a week ahead of them, Hennesey narrowed his eyes at a row of brown, jutting hills in their way and said, 'Them's the Chiricahuas, Seven. We're in Arizona now.'

'Let's celebrate by findin' a nice, shady spot and gettin' off and restin' a couple of hours.'

There was a narrow gorge with a spring-fed stream trickling through it high up in the Chiricahua Mountains. They got down from their horses near the spring to let the animals drink and graze for a while, and Seven stretched out in the shade of the gorge with his back resting against a cool, smooth stone that was more comfortable than any chair he'd ever leaned back against. 'This is more the way to live,' he sighed. 'I could work like this all week and never complain.'

Hennesey sat on his heels near Seven and tipped his hat low over his eyes. 'Take yourself forty winks, boy.'

'Why don't you knock of, too?'

'Well.' The sergeant pulled a piece of oak grass from the ground and put it between his teeth. 'These hills is named for Apaches. The army's keepin' them down some lately, but it still ain'twise for everybody to sleep at once in broad daylight jus' for the luxury of it.'

'I'll draw sticks with you to see who gets to sleep.'

'Okay.'

Seven picked up a twig near his right leg and broke it unevenly. He held the two ends in his fist and put his hand

39

in front of Hennesey. The sergeant drew the longest stick, and lay back with his hands cupping his head.

An hour later Hennesey sat up and stretched. 'Better get goin'. Those hay-burners've had enough vacation.'

Before they mounted the older man said, 'Boy, you've been foolin' with your unloaded gun and shootin' the other one fairly regular. Let's put you to a test. Pick yourself a target, and let's see you hit it in a hurry.'

'Fair enough.' Seven switched guns so that the loaded revolver was in his right-hand holster. There was a small pine tree clinging to the side of the gorge sixty feet away. He said, 'That pine cone in the tree over there.'

He drew and fired and a pine cone in the tree exploded into tiny pieces that showered down into the gorge.

Hennesey nodded. 'Not bad. Not too bad.'

They mounted and rode on through the gorge until it fanned out into awide, sloping plain before them. Seven said, 'I've been thinkin', Sergeant. There's a thing you ought to know.'

'Yeah?'

'Uh, huh. That pine cone I shot outta the tree. That wasn't the pine cone I was aimin' at.'


Flood's trail dropped south through the Dragoons and he skirted Tombstone evidently, for no one there had seen him. They got to Tombstone at straight-up noon, and were riding out by two o'clock. Seven said, 'Disappointin'. I'd always figured Tombstone was a real hell-raiser of a town. It was as quiet as any I've seen.'

'Short time ago it was rough as any man could care for. There was Buckskin Frank Leslie and Luke Short, Charlie Brown and others, not to mention the Earp boys and Bat Masterson around. But the mines went bust. That does it every time.'

'Wonder why Flood didn't go through there.'

'I put that question to Johnny Slaughter while you was off at the stable. Flood promised 'im one time he wouldn't show up in that town while Johnny was sheriff. One thing about Flood. If he likes you, he'll not go back on a thing he tells you.'

'How can you be sure he likes you?'

Hennesey grinned. 'That's the main question, all right. Also, he's been known to stop likin' people quite sudden.'

At a small trading post outside of Fort Huachuca, where the profit lay principally in a quick turnover in liquor, the two men crowded up to the short plank bar and ordered whiskey. After their second drink, Hennesey told the bar-tender-storekeeper, 'You sure do a fine business here.'

'Ain't al'ays so good.'

'What's the occasion?'

The bartender took in the dozen roughly dressed men in the room with a sweeping move of his head. 'All these fellas come over here hopin' to get a look at Jim Flood.'

'Oh yeah?' Hennesey pushed his glass over the counter. 'Wanna bring it t' life again.'

When the glass was refilled, he said, 'Flood's who I'm lookin' for Ol' friend. I tried a dozen places in the last five, six days and he hadn't been at none of 'em. He still around here?'

'Slept here last night. Gave 'im m' own bed, by God, an' I slept on the floor over there.'

'Expect 'im back?'

'Don't know. Doubt it. This mornin' he said he was goin' to visit a girl he recalled from last time he was down around the border here.'

'Betcha I know who he's athinkin' of,' an old man down the bar said, wagging his head gleefully. 'Betcha, Harry, he's athinkin' of that Hermosillo girl down to Santa Cruz. He and she was mighty thick one time.'

Outside, Seven said, 'We goin' to Santa Cruz?'

'Flood's got more'n one girl pinin' for 'im around here. We'check some more. If nothin' turns up, we'll head for Mexico.'

It was the afternoon of the following day that they crossed the border headed for Santa Cruz. 'I doubt we'll ever get

S.D.S—3  41

another glimpse of Jim Flood in our lifetimes,' Seven said, 'but at least I'm gettin' me a lot of sight-seein' done.' He'd fallen a few feet behind Hennesey and he called suddenly, 'Dammit! Wait a minute, will ya?' He got down from his roan and picked his Colt up from the ground, shaking sand from the barrel. 'I'm gettin' too fast for my own good with this empty gun. It got away from me.'

The sun settled down and at last disappeared behind the arid plains to their right. 'I'd guess we'll be to Santa Cruz around midnight,' Hennesey said.

It was a dark night. There was no moon, and long shreds of almost invisible clouds hid most of the stars in the sky.

At about ten o'clock Hennesey put his hand out and grabbed Seven by the shoulder. 'Stop.'

Seven looked at the dim outline of the man beside him. 'What's the matter?'

Within a few seconds he heard hoofbeats. A horse was racing swiftly somewhere in the dark to their left, and the pounding rhythm of sound grew, reaching a peak when the rider was nearest them, then faded quickly once more as the horse sped away into the north.

'That's what I call movin',' Seven said. 'He oughtta be in Montana come sunup.'

'Maybe Flood's in Santa Cruz after all,' Hennesey decided. 'And causin' some excitement.' He'd just finished speaking when they heard the new sound. It swelled out of the south like thunder, individual hoofbeats completely lost in the overall sound of rumbling, rushing horses.

'Sounds like a whole army,' Seven said.

'I think maybe, we better get out of its way,' Hennesey suggested.

They rode quickly at right angles from the charging horde bearing down upon them, and the moon chose that moment to push its uppermost edge over a ridge in the southwest.

There were perhaps fifty riders swarming over a hill at full speed. In the moon's silver haze several of the leading riders saw Seven and Hennesey. They shouted angrily in Spanish, and within a few seconds the large body of heavily armed

Mexicans were pulling up in prancing halts, forming a small circle around the rangers. Their leader was a finely dressed, scowling young man with narrow shoulders. He was the only man in the formidable group who was not armed. He snarled, 'Americanos!'

'I'm afraid you got the wrong party,' Hennesey said, his eyes moving steadily along the tight circle of gun muzzles pointed at him and Seven.

'Neither of these men are him, Senor Bastano,' one of the other men said.

'What does it matter?' a burly Mexican with crossed bandoleers over his chest demanded. 'They are gringos. Let us shoot them!'

Hennesey said, 'We're lawmen. We got nothin' to do with your fight.' He chose the calm older man to talk to. 'What's the excitement?'

The old man said, 'An American has lured Señor Bastano's wife from his bed. Then when two of the Senor's vaqueros found them together in Santa Cruz, the American shot them both.'

'I say shoot these two gringos, then chase the other one,' someone insisted and a low, raw murmur of agreement ran among them.

'That man's name Flood?' Hennesey asked, trying to change the subject.

'They know him!' the bandoleered man shouted.

'Shooting you,' Bastano told Hennesey, 'and the baby boy with you, will even the score for my vaqueros.' He turned his horse away. 'Kill them.'

A dozen hammers clicked back into firing position around them and Seven said loudly. 'Bastano is a coward not to do the shooting!'

The Mexican leader whirled his horse back around and rode over to Seven, his face white with fury. 'I would be pleased to do it myself! I am not carrying a gun!'

'Here!' Seven carefully lifted a Colt from his holster and, reaching over, shoved the gun into Bastano's belt. 'All right, let's see you fight this baby boy, mister.' He held his left

43

hand poised over his remaining Colt. I'll fight you left-handed!'

Bastano's face twisted with hate as he found himself jockeyed into a position of defending his personal honor. He did not reach for the revolver.

'I say you're scared to fight. Any man takes half a hundred men after a solitary fella who's stole his wife ain't much of a man.'

There was a whisper of voices as some of the men explained what Seven had said to the Mexicans who didn't understand English.

'These men won't follow a coward! Show 'em how brave you are!' Seven leaned forward, and his voice lashed out like a whip, 'Go ahead!'

Bastano ran his tongue over his lips, and a film of sweat broke out along his forehead. He whispered finally, 'I won't kill you. You didn't cause the trouble.'

Instinctively, timing his words, Seven waited through a few seconds of intense silence. 'Bastano is right,' he finally said. 'No need for killing. Let's go, Hennesey.'

Frowning, silent men cleared a path for them as they rode slowly out of the circle. When they'd left, the Mexicans a short distance behind them, Hennesey murmured, 'We better get ready to sprout wings. Somebody may notice that gun ain't loaded.'

They were a hundred yards away when a voice behind them shrieked in sudden rage and was lost in a general uproar of violent curses. They fled through the night as rifles began cracking behind them.

Seven leaned low, turning briefly from timeto time and shooting snap shots at the shadowy targets behind him. Twice when Hennesey fired, men plunged from their horses, and once both a horse and rider went down in a sprawling heap.

After a few minutes' run the already hard-worked Mexican horses began to fall farther behind. The rifle shots became fewer and at last stopped altogether. The rangers kept their gallop until it was safe to slow down and let their mounts get their breath.

Hennesey muttered, 'Never thought we'd be fightin' Flood's battles for 'im.' He grunted with amusement. 'You almost had me convinced you was a top gunhand back there. Poor ol' Bastano was like t' die of shock.'

'Me,' Seven said. 'I'm beginning to realize how nervous a man can get when he's in a spot where he's maybe gonna get killed. I'll bet I couldn't hit nothin' in a real fight.'

'Well, your shootin' is improved, anyhow, since you first shot at that rock in the river. You may have hit the wrong pine cone back there in the Chiricahuas, but at least you hit the right pine tree.'


## CHAPTER SEVEN

Now began a long trek north. They missed Flood at a ranch just over the border by only an hour. He'd evidently gone to Bisbee, and they were there two days trying to locate some sign of him. While there, Seven borrowed money from Hennesey to replace his missing Colt, and he also wrote a letter to Joy Harrington from the Delta Hotel. It took him half a day to write the letter, which said: 'My dear Miss Joy: I am well and hope this letter finds you the same. Sergeant Hennesey and me are having a hard time catching the man we are after. He is a very busy fellow, and we are always on the move but mostly in the wrong direction or too late because he mostly has been and gone already. But that is not the reason for writing to you and the reason is instead that I hope we will be back soon and I hope you and your father are well and happy and I think about you quite a bit. Sergeant Hennesey says to send his regards and etc. and etc. Sincerely yours, Seven Smith.'

The next day they read in the *Bisbee Chronicle* that James Flood had never been to Bisbee at all. Instead, he'd gone to Sonoita where he'd won a large sum at poker tables, had drunk a staggering amount of whiskey and dismantled two saloons. When he'd last been seen, he was heading roughly in the direction of Tucson.

'Let's go,' Hennesey said.

They rode out of Bisbee, and Seven never did get the telegraph message sent in care of the Delta Hotel. 'Have found out who you're following. Don't continue. Quit Rangers if necessary. Signed Joy Harrington.'

Twelve days later, near Sombrero Butte about fifty miles above Tucson, they talked to a cavalry lieutenant in charge of a squad policing the Galiuro Mountains for off-reservation Apaches. The lieutenant hadn't seen Jim Flood but he had talked to a Tucson businessman who was riding a painted pony to San Carlos. 'Fascinating man,' the cavalry officer said. 'He was telling me about a method they've recently developed back East for artificially causing a female sturgeon to produce eggs. I didn't quite follow the whole process, as it was fairly involved, but it sounded quite logical. The San Carlos lake is cold enough, and secluded enough that he feels he can successfully plant thousands of sturgeon minnows there. His reason for the trip just now is to check certain details about the lake. If all goes well, he'll stock the lake and keep the females producing eggs all year round, using this new method. And he thinks that within two or three years he'll have an excellent chance of cornering the world's caviar market.'

Hennesey nodded politely. 'That is interestin', Leiutenant.'

He glanced at Seven, and though there was not the least change of expression on either of their faces, they began to share Jim Flood's joke together.

'Apaches keepin' you busy these days?'

'Well, there are always some of them wandering off to raid and make trouble. I guess it will always be that way.'

'We'd best be movin' on. So long, Lieutenant.'

They moved north and northwest into an immense flat shelf of sun-baked earth, and as soon as they were out of hearing distance their pent-up laughter came out of them at the same time. Seven's laugh lasted much longer than Hennesey's, slowly working its way down to an occasional bubbling chuckle. Then, suddenly, his face began to grow serious. At last he said, 'You know, maybe – just maybe there is something to that sturgeon idea. I don't know much about that caviar stuff but the more you think of it, the more it sounds like the kind of thing some far-sighted fella might be doin' these days.'

Hennesey took off his hat long enough to brush his thick hair back. He put it on again and seemed to be considering an answer to Seven's statement. Instead, he began to whistle a low, tuneless song.

At San Carlos they continued their northerly direction, veering west through the Sierra Apache range and continuing ever north by way of the Tonto Basin and Mogollon Mesa.

Forty miles south of Flagstaff, after a day's ride through cold, cloudy weather, they made camp at a place where two small creeks forked into one, ten-foot-wide stream.

In the middle of the night Seven worked his eyes slowly open, vaguely uncomfortable. Descending from the dark night above him were thousands of softly turning particles of white.

He raised himself on an elbow. 'Hey, Hennesey. It's snowin'.'

The sergeant had pulled his hat far down over his face. He nodded his head slightly where it was resting in the seat of his saddle. 'Uh, huh.'

Seven got his own hat from beside him and imitated Hennesey.

In the morning a two-inch blanket of powdery white snow covered the camp.

'We'll be hittin' more and more into bad weather,' Hennesey observed. 'Won't be long afore November's behind us.'

Beyond Flagstaff they moved once more into wild country. They crossed the Little Colorado, moved over the Kaibito Plateau and eventually came to the wide Colorado.

47

'Reckon,' Hennesey said, 'that we are about in Utah at this point.'

'You'd think, havin' nothin' better to do, Flood'd head south for the bad months.' Seven pulled his big-collared coat closer around his face to offset a freezing north wind.

Later that day they found the first man they'd talked to in more than three weeks who had actually seen Flood. An old Navajo was living in a small canvas-covered wickiup not far from the bank of the Colorado.

When Hennesey had given him a few coins to help his memory, he recalled that a man named Flood had passed by the day before, and had crossed the river to head into the wild, uncharted land to the north where a distant range of mountains was covered with snow.

Two days later they rode through a snow-covered flat and started up the rolling foothills leading to the mountains beyond. It had snowed the entire day before, and now the sky was iron-gray overhead.

Hennesey breathed a long, deep sigh, and said, 'He must've finally gone plain loco. If we hadn't found the place he camped that first night, I'd say that Navajo told us two dollars' worth a' lies.'

Seven, numb with cold, was staring at the path ahead, helping to guide the roan so she wouldn't slip on the icy ground under the snow. 'Good thing we had these animals sharp shod back in whatever that last settlement was. Sure slippery goin'.'

And then it happened.

Wordlessly the sergeant, who had been studying the ridges dived out of his saddle toward Seven. His big hands grabbed at Seven's arm, and the younger man was instantly dragged off his horse. Hennesey's body seemed to crumple in mid-air, and Seven heard two distinct sounds. A solid plop, and a buzz as though an angry wasp had sped by near his ear. It was only after they were lying in the snow on the ground that Seven heard the two shots, one hard on the other. The shots were dim and muffled by distance. Seven stared at a faraway ridge. He saw a horseman silhouetted against the sky there

48

for a fraction of a second. And then the horseman was gone.

Seven turned to Hennesey who was lying near him on his side. 'Hennesey,' he whispered, suddenly remembering the awful plop of sound he'd heard. 'Hennesey!' He reached out and took the sergeant by the shoulder, and at his touch the other man rolled onto his back, one hand falling loosely at his side.

'Oh, my God!' Seven murmured.

The sergeant had been hit in the middle of the chest, and glistening blood was beginning to stain and dampen the thick coat he was wearing. His lips twitched then, and his eyelids moved faintly, staying shut.

Seven got to his knees above the wounded man and with shaking fingers, unbuttoned the coat and shirt and underwear to get at the bullet hole. It was a raggedly round puncture only the size of a small thimble, but it was bleeding in quick, nervous spurts. Seven took out his bandanna and held it against the wound. Then he took off his belt and wrapped it around Hennesey's chest, buckling it tight enough to hold the bandage firm and keep the blood from pouring out. 'I'll get a fire goin',' he whispered, half to the sergeant, half to himself. 'Get you warm.'

There were few trees around, and those were wet and frozen. It took Seven half an hour to start a small fire. He put some other firewood near the flames to let it begin to dry from the heat, then he moved the sergeant so that the warmth was close to him. He touched the bandage to see if blood was soaking through, and found the outside of the bandanna still dry. Seven got Hennesey's bedroll down from behind the bay's saddle and unrolled it near the sergeant. It was while he was doing this that he realized he was crying. No sound, no change of expression. Simply tears.

He brushed his face with his hand and knelt down to try to decide how best to get Hennesey into the bedroll.

The sergeant opened his eyes and looked at Seven.

Seven tried to grin and sound reassuring. 'You stopped bleedin'.'

Hennesey's lips did not move. His face was calm and relaxed and his eyes stayed on Seven. The younger man said, 'If you hadn't pulled me off my horse, I'd've got hit right in the head.'

Then the eyes shut and Hennesey died.

Seven leaned over and gripped the man's shoulders hard, trying to force some of his own life into the sergeant's big body, but it was no good. Finally he let go and sat down beside Hennesey and lowered his face into his hands.

The fire was almost completely out when Seven stood up at last. He put a few more pieces of wood on it and built it up a little. It started to snow as he explored the land around him. He selected a spot at the crest of a nearby hill from which he could look down over the edge of Utah and see the country that was Arizona on the horizon.

Taking the small hand axe he'd chopped firewood with, he began chipping at the frozen ground on the hill crest.

The next day at noon the sun was shining and he had hollowed out a grave, working straight through except for a few hours during the night. He took his belt from Hennesey's chest, and took the sergeant's bandanna in place of his own. He went through his friend's pockets and put the money he found, a few letters and a pocket watch in the sergeant's saddlebags. Then he picked the big man up, carried him to the grave and placed him in it. Then he said. 'No. No, I guess not. A man oughtn't to be put to rest with his guns on,' and he unstrapped Hennesey's guns.

Three hours later, he'd erected a rough wooden cross over the grave. He'd found a thick log and split a smooth, wide piece out of it for a headboard. After some thought, he'd laboriously burned a few words into the wood with a hot iron. Then he'd nailed the headpiece to the upright part of the cross with two horseshoe nails.

The bay and the roan nuzzled snow aside to see what feed they could find while Seven broke camp. Finally, he swung to saddle and the two horses and rider moved past the grave. Before moving on up into the higher hills where he had seen

Flood, Seven took one last look at the words on the cross and decided they were as fitting as he could make them.

Hennesey 1884
Welcome him God
He was a man

## CHAPTER EIGHT

Seven rode hard and fast to narrow the distance between him and the man somewhere in the hills ahead. He found tracks that hadn't been completely snowed over at the ridge from which Hennesey had been shot, and he followed them the rest of the day and well into the bright, moonlit night. He slept from midnight to three o'clock, mostly to give the horses some rest, then moved on again. Alone now, he quickly adopted Hennesey's habit of watching far ahead and scanning the land to each side of him, with an occasional necessary glance at the route directly before him. Instinctively now, perhaps unconsciously aware that the sergeant had done so, he slowed before topping high points in the land, moving up slow and studying the country ahead before outlining himself against the sky.

And that is why, after two days of pushing himself at a killing pace, he saw Flood before Flood saw him.

Seven's roan was edging upward from the bottom of a gulley and when only the Ranger's hat was visible to anyone beyond the gulley, he saw a tiny black speck moving around the side of a mountain in the distance and pulled the mare to a halt. Dismounting, he went on foot to where he could cautiously watch the faraway horseman. When Flood was once more out of sight, he got on the roan and led the bay in a breakneck, plunging run through the snowdrifts and frozen waste leading to the mountain. It was about a four-mile run to where Flood had disappeared, and by the time Seven got there the horses were blowing so frantically he was afraid their breathing would warn Flood. The roan crashed chest-deep through one last drift of snow, her hoofs sending plumes of white sailing into the air, and Seven pulled the exhausted animal to a halt in a clearing where wind had swept the ground almost clear of snow. The bay coming up behind ran into the roan blindly, and they both almost went down.

Seven pulled his Winchester and went up the mountain on foot, slipping and sliding on the way. Slowing down as he started angling around the slope he was on, he tried to control his own rapid, heavy breathing and calm the furious beating of his heart.

Then he saw Flood, and he dropped instantly to the ground, half-burying himself in the snow. Flood's back was to him, he was riding his pinto up a narrow ledge more than a thousand feet away. The ledge moved up from the base to the top of a steep five-hundred-foot slope. Flood was more than halfway to the top.

Seven swung his rifle to his shoulder, elbowing up out of the snow a little. His right hand was so cold the trigger finger was stiff and jerky in its movements, and Seven put the finger in his mouth to warm it, then stuck the hand under his coat and wiped the warmed finger on his shirt. He aimed very carefully at the middle of Flood's back. And then he squeezed the trigger.

Something slammed so powerfully against his left shoulder that it spun him completely around in the snow, and the rifle flew from his fingers. He numbly realized that somehow he had been shot, and his right hand went to the wound, holding it hard. He blinked snow from his eyes and looked back at the ledge. Flood's pinto was rearing and fighting, and as Seven watched, the big paint slipped on the icy ledge and went off into space with Flood still in the saddle. Rider and mount fell thirty feet before hitting the steep slope in an explosive burst of flying snow, then plunged and rolled separately but never far from each other, down the long, steep slope. Seven realized vaguely that Flood's foot was caught in the stirrup. Twisting and turning through their long whirling fall, they at last hit bottom and were almost buried in a drift while several avalanches of hissing snow that they had started cascaded down upon them.

There was no movement where the horse and rider lay at the foot of the high slope.

Seven looked at his shoulder, but there was no way of telling how badly he was hurt. The arm of his coat, high up toward the shoulder, was torn. There was still no sign of blood seeping through the cloth.

Getting to his feet, Seven pulled the rifle from the snow and ran awkwardly down the mountain, holding the gun in one hand. At a steep point his feet went out from under him and he slid forty feet on his rump, holding the Wichester up to protect it. The slide pulled his britches out of his boots and icy melting snow got into the boot tops, but he didn't notice. At the foot of the mountain he plowed through deep snowdrifts for two hundred yards, at last coming to a halt near the foot of the slope where Flood had fallen.

The big pinto was only visible from the withers up, and the horse's head was turned grotesquely, its neck broken. Seven saw the outline of a man's body, all of it but one protruding boot covered with a thick dusting of snow. Holding his cocked rifle in his right hand, Seven stuck a toe under the man and raised him an inch or two, then got his heel against the man's side and pushed him over onto his back.

Flood was unconscious, but he was breathing. Seven searched him quickly and thoroughly, holding his rifle pinched between his upper arm and his chest. One of Flood's six-guns was missing, and Seven shoved the other into his own belt. He found a long, viciously sharp knife in one of the man's boots, and an over-and-under Deringer in his jacket pocket. Then he stepped back to really look at the man for the first time.

Flood was big and smoothly muscled. His face was relaxed and calm, and his features were fine. He had thick, curling black hair, and Seven noticed a thin white scar that ran across Flood's high forehead just underneath the hairline. The man was expensively dressed. Seven had seen a pair of boots in Flagstaff similar to those Flood was wearing. They were made especially in Massachusetts to fit one particular man, and they'd been priced at eighty dollars. Flood wore a string tie, and a heavy gold watch chain was strung across his vest. His coat was lighter than most Seven had seen. It was of a soft, half-shiny material and it looked as if it would keep the cold out.

Flood's right arm moved, his fingers coming together as though to close on the handle of a gun, and then he opened his eyes that were blue and clear. The eyes whipped over Seven, instantly taking in the hurt arm and the cocked Winchester. He turned his head slightly from side to side in the bank of snow it was resting on and said in a voice curiously combining softness and strength, 'Where the hell's my hat?'

Seven raised the Winchester to a steady level at Flood's head. He tried to keep the tremble of sorrow and fury out of his voice. 'Mister, you killed a friend of mine. I been ridin' almost straight forty-eight hours to shoot your head clear off.'

Flood frowned. 'You're one of those two fellas who was trailing me just over the Utah border?'

'That's right.'

Shaking his head, Flood said, 'Jesus. If I missed one of those shots, I deserve to die.' He ignored the Winchester, gazing instead with waitful amusement into Seven's eyes. 'Fire away.'

The muzzle of the barrel fell a fraction of an inch and Seven hitched the rifle higher, resting his finger firmly on the trigger. But he couldn't bring himself to fire.

I wish you'd make up your mind,' Flood said in a pleasant, conversational tone. 'The suspense is awful.'

Seven could feel tears of rage and disgust with himself brimming into his eyes. He willed his finger to pull back a fraction of an inch so that the hammer would fall, but nothing happened. A force he couldn't understand, that seemed to be lodged in the curved finger itself, stubbornly kept him from shooting.

He backed away and sat down on a snow-covered rock,

54

his Winchester resting over his knees and still pointing at Flood.

'Now that that's over,' the man said, 'what about my horse?'

'Dead. Neck broken.'

'Damn.' Flood sighed. 'One of the best horses a man ever had. That shot you took at me burned 'im across the butt. That's how come he got excited an' slipped. Looks like the potshot I took at you didn't go too far wide of the mark.'

Seven's arm was beginning to burn painfully, but he noticed that with the numbness gone, he could control his fingers, and some strength was coming back into the muscles.

Flood sat up and put his hand into his jacket pocket.

Seven said, 'I got your Deringer.'

The outlaw took a cigar from the pocket. Miraculously, it was in perfect shape. 'Last one. Want half?'

The Ranger ignored him and he thumbed a match to light the smoke.

'Believe me, fella, I wouldn't shoot you under any conditions. My leg is all banged to hell. Maybe broken. I can't move it. And my horse is dead. I would get somewhat cold lyin' here all winter. So—' He blew out a small cloud of cigar smoke. 'I need you. Would you mind tellin' me what plans you got, if any?'

'I'm goin' to take you back to Texas so they can hang you.'

'Texas? You follow me from clear out there?'

'Yeah. Couple of times we thought you knew.'

Flood shook his head. 'Never paid attention particularly. There's usually so many fellas followin' me that I don't bother counting 'em.' He brought his left leg up under him and stood up briefly, but the right leg was as loose and helpless to him as an empty pantleg. He sat back down. 'How you fixed horsewise?'

'You can ride Hennesey's bay.'

Flood took the cigar out of his mouth and looked at Seven with eyes that were for the first time thoroughly serious. 'Hennesey?' He put his left leg down slowly. 'You with the Rangers?'

'Yes.'

Flood frowned at the cigar in his hand. 'I guess this is the first time shootin' somebody else hurt me about as much as it did him.'

'You ain't dead and buried in the frozen ground back there! You ain't hurt so much!' Seven stood up. 'The horses is back around the mountain and I ain't leavin' you here alone. So you're goin' to walk or crawl or somethin' to come along with me.'

'Okay. First, do you mind if we take a look at this leg? If it's busted, I'd like to tie it up some before takin' any hikes.'

Seven, angry and unsure of himself, raised his hurt left arm and rubbed his face, finding small, icy lines on his cheeks that were frozen tears. 'All right. Look at your leg.'

Flood rolled up his pantleg. 'None of the damned thing is too good,' he muttered, 'but it's around the ankle where she's worst.'

He leaned far forward, the cigar jutting from one corner of his mouth, and pulled the boot from his foot, his face going tight-set against the pain. The sock came with the boot and Seven could see that the ankle and foot were both blue and swollen far beyond normal size.

'I'll never get that boot back on till the swellin' goes down,' Flood decided, probing at the injured area, 'but I'll be damned if I ain't still in one piece. Don't think any bones went. Just bruised, battered and twisted all to hell.' His strong exploring fingers felt carefully up past his knee and to the thigh. 'All okay. Guess God looks out for us idiots who go around rollin' down mountains.' He looked at Seven and said, 'By the way, you know who I am. Who are you?'

'Name's Smith. Seven Smith.'

'Well look, Smith. I hate like hell to be a nuisance, but would you get the blanket off my paint? I'll rip a piece off it to wrap this foot in. I'd just as soon not lose it.'

Keeping an eye on the outlaw, Seven went to the dead horse and kicked away the snow covering it. As he leaned down to untie the bedroll behind the saddle, Flood called. 'I may as well mention in good faith that there's a gun in that bedroll. Just so's you'll know I'm not tryin' to play tricks on you.'

Taking the bedroll apart, Seven found the gun, a .44 Smith & Wesson, and added it to his growing collection. He took the blanket to where Flood was waiting and tossed it to him. 'I'll get you somethin' to use as a cane.'

'Thanks.'

While the other man tore a strip from the thick wool blanket and began turning it around his foot, Seven tried to find a piece of wood he could use as a crutch. There was nothing he could see close by, and the nearest trees were more than half a mile away. He went back to the dead pony and took Flood's rifle from the holster. Emptying it, he took it over to the man and dropped it beside him. 'You can lean on that.' He added, realizing as he spoke that his words were unnecessary, 'It ain't loaded.'

Flood tied the end of the wool strip and looked up. 'I suspected that.' He took the rifle and started to shift up to his one good leg, then sat back down. 'Long as we're bein' so medical-minded, it wouldn't hurt to take a look at the place you got shot.'

'It ain't much, or I couldn't use my arm.'

'Better take your coat off and see. I been shot eight times, mostly shallow hits, and I can tell you there's nothin' more bothersome than an untended shot wound.'

Seven backed away, leaned his Winchester over a rock and shrugged out of his coat.

'Don't take your shirt off or you'll get too cold. Just cut enough of a slit in the cloth to see your hurt.'

Seven did as Flood said. 'It's almost nothin'. Just grazed me. But it knocked me clear around when it hit.'

'Bullets do funny things. Take some snow and rub the cut out with it good. Better yet, come'ere and let me do it for you.' Flood waited for an answer. 'Come on, God damn it!'

57

Seven picked up his rifle and went over to the other man. The gun muzzle was resting directly against Flood's chest as he leaned down before the outlaw. 'Don't you try nothin', mister.'

Flood took a handful of clean snow and rubbed the wound so hard that blood started to flow again. He took a clean white handkerchief from his pocket and wrapped it around the arm, tying it firmly. 'Take the cloth off it in an hour or two. It'll be all right. Won't fester.'

'Let's go.'

Flood leaned forward, shifting his weight to push himself up on his left leg with the aid of the rifle. When he stood up, even though he was leaning on the rifle, Flood still stood taller than Seven. Seven, swinging his eyes around for one last look at the ground, saw an inch-long line of black breaking the snow a few feet away. He walked to it and pulled out a wide, curling-brimmed black hat. He handed it to Flood and the big outlaw flipped it expertly in his hand so that the snow came off and it took its right shape once more.

'Go on,' said Seven. 'Back around the mountain.'

Holding the top of the barrel near his waist, swinging from the rifle butt to his left foot, Flood started back along the bottom of the steep slope. Even at the disadvantage of the awkward, hopping motion, he moved with sureness and a certain grace startling in a man so large. Just once he slipped. The rifle butt shot out from under him on a glassy slant of ice under the snow and he fell with all his weight, slamming the injured foot hard against the rocklike surface beneath him. Seven, walking behind him, knew that the fall hurt terribly, but there was no hint of pain from Flood. He said, with mild irritation, 'Damn!' and started to get up. Seven helped him stand, and he went on as though nothing had happened.

At the clearing where the horses were, Flood looked the animals over and said, 'What you been feedin' them poor beasts?'

'They been makin' do.'

'They're both underweight a hundred pounds. Good horses can't go on the same food as a little wild mustang, Smith.'

Seven was leading the horses to where Flood stood. 'I know it!' he said. 'I ain't starvin' them outta meanness. Ran out of grain a while back and couldn't give 'em much even before it was gone. We was busy followin' you and couldn't go t' town any time we pleased so's we could travel in style!'

Flood studied the sky where the dim, settling sun was a pale haze behind banks of clouds. 'All things considered, do you mind if I make a suggestion?'

'What?'

'These horses ain't in too good shape, and we're in for a roarer of a storm. Probably tonight. I'd give our chances of gettin' out of these hills as about one out of three. Poor odds. My idea is this. Let's go on the way I was headin'. I got a cabin about a three-hour ride from here. Was goin' there to sit out the winter in quiet and peace. It's well stocked.'

'Nope.'

'You'd be wise to reconsider.'

Seven took the rifle and two revolvers from Hennesey's horse and put the guns with his own gear on the roan. 'Can you get on the bay by yourself?'

Flood grabbed the pommel with his left hand and sprang with his left foot to the stirrup. Shoving his empty rifle into the saddle holster, he pulled his right leg over the horse's rear with his right hand. As Seven swung aboard the roan, Flood said, 'If you wanta ride back around, it occurs to me there's a couple of thousand dollars in my saddlebags. Suit yourself.'

Seven nodded. 'Guess so. You ride ahead. And don't bother tryin' to find shells for your rifle any place in the bay's gear. Got 'em all on my horse.'

Flood laughed. 'Any differences of opinion we probably have about goin' to Texas are second rate considerations right now. Our present problem, Smith, is the weather.'

They arrived at the base of the steep slope and Seven stripped the big paint of its saddlebags and threw them over the roan's neck. He'd noticed, in digging away the snow, that the paint's saddle was an elegant make, with fine silver-work on it. 'That saddle must be worth a lot of money, Flood. I can tie it on the bay's back.'

'No. It belonged on the stallion. It was fitted perfect to his back. He could've worn it all year round, never took it off, and never got a saddle sore. And it looked handsome on him. Leave it.'

Near nightfall they were three miles back along the way they'd come when the snow started again. It fell in vast waves of immense flakes that piled up swiftly into freezing, deadly drifts. Seven couldn't find a place to camp where they wouldn't be buried by morning. At last he called ahead to Flood. 'I hope you ain't lyin' about that cabin.'

Flood wheeled the bay mare around, her legs swirling the deep snow. 'I'm surely glad you're not as stubborn and dumb as I was beginnin' to think you were.'

CHAPTER NINE

It was almost morning when they came to the cabin which was good-sized and solidly built, tucked back in a half-circle of ground surrounded on three sides by a winding forty-foot cliff that protected it from drifting snow. Behind the cabin there was a big lean-to. Nearly frozen and numb from exhaustion, Seven followed Flood into the lean-to and slid from the beaten roan who stood with her legs far apart, her head far down.

'You'd decided an hour later to change directions, I doubt we'd have made it,' Flood said, disengaging his left foot from the stirrup and going down off the right side of the bay who was too exhausted to even be curious about the unfamiliar maneuver. He pulled the empty rifle from the bay and leaned on it. Seven said, 'Move over to the wall. I ain't about to have my head busted by that gun.'

When Flood was out of reach, Seven stripped the horses. He took a hoofpick from his saddlebag and pried ice and snow from their hoofs. The frog on the bay's hind right was torn and sensitive but the hurt was not serious. He put the hoof down gently. 'Feed in the house?'

'Yes.' Flood turned and made his way toward the cabin and Seven, rifle in hand, followed him.

The cabin was bitterly cold but its walls were well chinked and its one window was set in properly so no draft came from it. There was one large room with a fireplace. Two smaller rooms, a supply room and tack room, led off to one side.

Flood pointed to the supply room. 'Feed's in there. You want to build a fire or tend the horses?'

Seven took off his hat and slapped it against his pants to get the snow off. 'Far as I can see, I'll have to do both.'

Flood lowered himself into a rocking chair near the fireplace and sighed happily. 'Guess you're right. You can't let me go out where the guns are. And you can't leave me in here, 'cause for all you know, I got a couple of cannons hid in the shack.'

'Have you?'

Flood nodded at an old flintlock above the fireplace. 'That's the extent of my arsenal. Frankly, I wouldn't trust it for anythin' but decoration, Barrel's rusted.'

Leaving the door wide open, Seven went into the supply room and dipped two buckets of oats from a big metal container. Carrying them both in one hand and the gun in the other, he went back into the main room. 'Let's go.'

'Smith, there are no guns in here.' Flood turned in the chair and faced him. 'I am stayin' here and buildin' a fire. I don't guess you'll shoot me unless I try somethin' more violent than that.'

'I can wallop you with a gun barrel.'

'No.' Flood shook his head. 'More, I don't think you'd try. Go on to the animals. I won't cause you any trouble.'

61

Seven hesitated, then went out of the cabin. Once outside, he put the buckets down and hurried quietly around to the window. It was now light enough for him to see into the room. Flood had left the rocker and was kneeling at the fireplace on his one good knee, his hurt leg stretched out behind him and to his side. He was breaking twigs from the firewood stacked beside the chimney.

When Seven got back from the lean-to, a small fire was burning and the room was quickly warming up. Flood was back in the rocking chair, his injured foot stretched out toward the flames before him. Ice that had formed on the stiffened bandage was melting and the wool glistened in the firelight.

'How's the foot?' Seven shut the door behind him.

'I am pleased to report that it hurts like hell. I was afraid it was frozen, those last two or three miles.'

Seven had left his Winchester along with the other gear in the open, shed-like affair where the horses were. He had left one Colt there too, and wore only one revolver. He'd brought cooking equipment and he said, 'I'll heat some coffee and jerky.'

'There's canned tomatoes and stuff there in the supply room,' Flood told him. 'And you oughtta bring those guns in. They'll rust.'

'They're oiled against the weather.'

Flood shrugged his shoulders.

Realizing he should have done so before, Seven went over the entire cabin, carefully looking for concealed weapons while the coffee and meat were making pleasant warming noises in the fireplace. There was, as Flood had said, no gun aside from the ancient flintlock over the mantel.

Eating later, he said, 'How come you got a place like this to come to? Must be a hundred miles from the nearest town.'

'Hundred and ten, unless somebody's put up a couple of buildings someplace and called it a town since last I was around here.' Flood glanced around him with detached eyes. 'I built this place when I was a kid.'

'All by yourself?'

'Uh-huh.'

'Lotta' work.'

'Took me two summers to get enough wood out here to build with. Three more to put it up.'

'What did you want to be so alone for?'

'Don't know. Just did.' Flood set his steaming coffee cup down on the floor and began to unwrap the bandage around his foot. 'Wool's softened up enough to take it off.' He stripped the last part of the bandage off the now nearly black foot and tossed the long line of cloth into the fire. 'Yep. It hurts enough that it'll be all right. Body's fightin' a battle to set things right down there. There's cigars someplace in the supply room. In an airtight box. Why don't you get 'em for us?'

'Okay.' Seven found the box and brought it back to the fireplace. He took a burning stick from the fire and lit two cigars and passed one to Flood.

'Back in those days,' the outlaw said, 'I wasn't on good terms with the human race, but I hadn't completely severed relations, either.'

Seven took a long, luxurious drag on his cigar. 'When did you cut off relations?'

'Oh, no particular time. It happened over quite a while. A little bit here, a little bit there. I was workin' in Durango one night when a barn burned down. There was quite a few pups in the barn – couple weeks old litter. I got there in time to grab a couple of 'em and run out. They was just about dead.

'A fat young couple had come up to watch the blaze, and as I come out, the girl kinda' giggled and waddled up close against the fella and said, 'Oh, I can't stand to see them burned things!' Right then I was ashamed and disgusted and felt like killin' the whole human race. In a minute another girl come up and took a look at the pups. She didn't say nothin'. She just took one of 'em and held it in her arms and dropped her shawl over it to keep the night wind off it,

63

and she whispered sort of low and sweet into its ear, and she start weepin' a little, as is a woman's right.

'One minute I wanted to kill everybody. The next minute I wanted to take the whole world into my arms and love it.

'Lots of wanted men claim somethin' horrible happened to drive 'em into always bein' in trouble.' Flood shook his head. 'Billy the Kid said he'd killed his first man defendin' his mother's honor. Billy was the biggest liar in New Mexico.

'Anyway, nothin' happened to me except about a thousand little things that rubbed me the wrong way. Seemed like for every decent person I bumped into there was a hundred towns full of cheap crooks, liars, braggarts and bullies. And then one day the greatest idea I ever had come to me.'

Seven finished his coffee and put the cup down on the floor. 'What?'

'To do exactly what I wanted for the rest of my life! We only get one apiece, you know.' Flood smiled at the fire. 'I decided never to give a damn about what other people thought, or to give a damn about the law or anything else. If I wanted to raise hell, take some money, have a woman, kill a man – why, I'd just God damn well right do it. Or if I want to help people, I do it, though I find that don't happen so often as the other things.'

'That's a light view of things,' Seven muttered. 'Especially killin'.'

Flood put his hands behind his head, leaning far back in the rocking chair. 'Killing ain't so serious. There's millions of people kickin' around this earth and a few more or less don't make any difference at all in the big picture. And everybody's got to die soon or late.' He grinned. 'Everybody but me, that is. I'll never die.'

Seven shook his head. 'Someplace in Texas there's a rope that says different.' He flicked his cigar ashes into the fireplace. 'Another thing about killin'. Aside from the dead, there's other people you hurt.'

'Hell! The saddest gal in the world has trouble rememberin' her boy friend's face two months after he's underground. That's why photographic saloons are coinin' the silver. Helps folks remember what they're wailin' about. No man is missed for long.'

Seven stood up and gathered the pots and pans to take them over to the table at one side of the room. As he put them down, he heard a rifle lever worked behind him. He drew his Colt as fast as he could, whirling around and ducking.

Flood was staring at him with amused eyes. The empty rifle was in his hands. 'Just thought I'd take a look at the inside of the barrel. Probably needs cleanin'.'

'You watch out or you'll get shot!' Seven said angrily. 'I ain't yet forgot Hennesey, and I'd just as leave shoot you as watch you hang!'

'I told you once how I felt about that man,' Flood said, his voice low and firm. 'There is a scar high on my forehead where a Comanche brave started to take my scalp ten years ago. It was Hennesey who stopped him. I don't want to be reminded again that I shot him.'

'Ain't you forgettin' who's runnin' this show?'

Flood levered the Winchester's bolt shut and reached out to lean the gun against the fireplace. 'Let's understand each other. I stopped needing you as soon as I got on that bay. Since then there hasn't been twenty minutes pass that I couldn't have gone my own way. But to do that, I'd have had to kill you. I didn't. Partly because you showed me certain kindnesses even though I'd killed your friend. Partly because I feel a debt to Hennesy, and you're the only one now that I can pay it to.'

'God!' Seven shoved his revolver back in its holster. 'And you were talkin' about dislikin' boastful fellas! You ain't had one chance to do me damage since you went down the mountain!' He turned back toward the pots and pans with disgust and instantly there was a solid thump from the door five feet to his right. He started nervously, his eyes swinging to the door and his mouth opening with surprise. There was a small hatchet buried deep in the wood.

'If you will examine that door,' Flood said acidly, 'you'll find a knothole about three inches above your head. You were too blind to see the hatchet, and too stupid to figure there might be one in the woodbox. I got it while you were walkin' around the cabin to look in at me through the window.' He leaned back in the rocker. 'I just give you that as a for example.'

His nerves tight, Seven took his gun out again. Holding it cocked and pointed at Flood, he used his other hand to search the man once more. 'I'll be more careful from now on.'

'I should hope so.'

Seven examined the tack room. It was nothing more than a large closet with a few bridles and halters hanging from its walls and an old saddle tossed in one corner.

He laid bedding out on the floor and went back to where Flood was sitting in the rocker. 'I'm lockin' you in that room over there. It's time we got some sleep.'

The outlaw reached for his rifle and got up. 'I could use a nap all right.'

Before Seven shut the door to the tack room he handed Flood an additional blanket. 'In case you want to wrap the foot in it.'

'Obliged.'

'And, Flood—'

'Yeah?'

The words came hard and Seven felt like a fool. 'Thanks for not hittin' me with that hatchet.'

'It's nothin'.'

Seven shut the door and forced it tightly closed with a long, thick log from the woodbox. Then, instead of sleeping on the bunk at one side of the room, he laid his bed out near the tack room door so that any disturbance of the log or door would wake him. He went to sleep with his revolver in easy reach. On edge as he was, he was even more exhausted, and he slept soundly, without a dream.

# CHAPTER TEN

It was late in the afternoon when Seven opened his eyes. He got up and stretched and found that his shoulder was stiff and sore from the bullet nick. After building the fire up, he went outside for a bucket of snow to make coffee. He gave grain to the horses and washed the dirty dishes with snow. Then he took the hatchet from the door and went to a clump of trees outside to cut a stout branch for Flood to use as a cane.

When he opened the door to the tack room, Flood was lying with his eyes wide open.

'Want some coffee?'

'Sure.' Flood sat up. 'Been lyin' here listenin' to you get the work done. And thinkin'.' He reached for the rifle.

'Here. Got a stick for ya'.' Seven handed him the cut branch and took the rifle.

Flood said, 'That's practically a two-dollar walkin' cane.' He got up and tested his weight on the jutting eight-inch grip at the top. 'Got a handle and everything.' He went to the rocking chair near the fire, and Seven knew he'd noticed the hatchet was gone.

'Left it outside.'

Flood laughed. 'Good idea. You'll need it out there for choppin' wood.'

Later, while Seven was cleaning the rifle, Flood said, 'A thing's been botherin' me some. Why in hell did the Rangers send a raw recruit like you after me? When folks chase after me, they usually do it in posses. But to send only two fellas, and one of 'em an amateur – it's surprisin'. – Even insultin'.'

Seven put a small piece of oiled cloth through the eye of the ramrod and shoved it down the barrel. 'I can see now that the lieutenant – he runs Company D – figured I'd get myself killed off. But I'm agoin' to take you back to Texas and ram you down his throat.'

Chuckling, Flood leaned down and put some more wood on the fire. 'You youthful fellas can't be beat for optimism. I don't know about him, but I don't ram too easy.'

'You know what I mean.'

'What's a Ranger boss want one of his boys dead for?'

Seven squinted through the barrel to see how it looked. 'Well, it's a sort of a private matter.'

'Girl, huh? What about Hennesey? Your boss want him to get shot too?'

'Hard to say. The sergeant was the only one who never got called for not sayin' sir to Herly.'

'Walt Herly?'

'Yeah.' Seven snapped the cleaned rifle shut and leaned it against the wall. 'How'd you know?'

'Knew him when he was a sheriff or marshal or some such in Texas. A fair gunhand, with the soul of a cockroach.'

'He always goes strictly by the book. But I'm startin' to see that a man like that can read the book most any way that pleases him best.'

'That, Smith, is the feelin' that is the first step towards outlawry. Maybe I can make a fair badman outa you while we're cooped up here.'

'Not me.' Seven grinned.

'You can do more livin' in one year of rampaging wild than most folks do in a whole lifetime.' Flood grinned back at Seven. 'Come on. I'll make you a junior partner in my firm.'

'Nope, not me. Truth is, I got a kind of a feelin' for the law. Somebody's got to stand for the right.'

'Speakin' of that,' Flood nodded at the guns on Seven's belt, 'you better learn to handle those things better or you won't be standin' for anything.'

'I'm not as bad as I used to be. I've been practicing off and on for six months.'

'In that case, you ain't got a natural feel for it.' Flood got up and went to the window. Leaning an elbow on the window sill and staring out at the snow, he said, 'That don't mean you can't win gunfights. It just means you got to recognize your limits and act accordin' to them.'

Seven got a piece of wood from the firebox and began to whittle absently. 'What do you mean?'

'I mean you got to figure on goin' into a fight with your gun in hand. Or you got to trick folks or some such. Don't never count on a draw like the one you made last night keepin' you out of a narrow grave.'

'God damn it,' Seven grumbled, 'I thought I was gettin' pretty good.'

Flood breathed on the window and drew a little smiling face with his fingertip on the fogged pane. 'You make a fine cup of coffee, anyway.' He lay down on the bed near the window and eased his bad foot up onto the blankets. 'I just knew one fella who was cut-and-dried faster with a gun than me. He wasn't worth a damn any other way, but he was greased lightnin' with his side pieces.'

'To be honest, I never heard of anybody who was claimed to be faster than you, Flood.'

'This fella, name of Sutton, didn't live long enough to make any kind of a reputation.' Flood put his hands back under his head. 'He was kind of loco. He'd holed up some-wheres for nearly three years just to practice every day at unholsterin' and shootin' them guns of his. And he had a gambler's quick hand. It was sight to see that day he shot down the sheriff in Wells Falls. I was watchin' the duel from a saloon window. Soon as the smoke cleared, Sutton let it be known that he was lookin' for me next. He was out to build himself up in a hurry. Prob'ly was anxious to have one of them Eastern publishing places do a penny dreadful about 'im.'

'So what happened?' Seven sliced a long slender sliver of wood from the stick and put it between his lips.

'I sent word to 'im that I was tied up, but that I'd meet him alone on Clancy Street at ten o'clock that night. At ten, he came walkin' along to where I was standing sort of in the shadows. I called him by name and his hand moved so quick you couldn't see it. He died with the most surprised look on his face you ever saw.'

69

Seven frowned, puzzled.

'I blew 'im in half with a sawed-off shotgun I was holdin' cocked and ready at my side.' Flood laughed at the ceiling. 'Sutton's expression was a thing to see, I tell you.'

'Do you think that was right, what you did?'

'I know damned well it was right. Like the fella says, they don't give you no prize for second place.'

'Poor ol' Sutton.' Flood shook his head and started to laugh again, his amusement so genuine and thorough that Seven found himself smiling too.

It snowed for nearly three days without stopping. But then, freakishly, an almost summer sun appeared and began its slow, steady work of unclogging the passes and filling the rivers leading to the sea. A hundred feet from the cabin a small creek of clear water that was like liquid ice came to life.

'Look,' Flood said, 'when the snow's gone, that creek'll be gone too. How 'bout it, jailer? Can I take me a bath in it, so's I can go back to Texas fresh and dainty?'

'If you're crazy enough to do that, it's okay with me.'

Flood hobbled out expertly, putting a little weight on his healing ankle and foot. He stripped himself at a place where the sun had dried a patch of earth, and hopped into the three-foot-deep, icy stream and sat down. 'Jesus Christ!' he bellowed, 'this is cool!' He ducked under altogether, then tossed his head back up, his gleaming black hair throwing a wide spray of water. He hopped out a moment later, slapping the water from his muscular shoulders and chest and his flat stomach. 'Seven!' he panted, 'you oughtta do that. It'll keep you healthy for a year – or kill you instantly.'

'Okay.' Seven tossed him a blanket to towel himself off. 'I'll take the spot upstream here.'

Thirty feet away, he took off his gun and put it on a rock extending out into the stream so that it would be at hand. Undressing, he stepped in. 'Hell, this ain't so cold as I thought,' he called to Flood. When he sat down in it, he realized why. His nerves were numbed, his body nearly paralyzed by the fiery cold. 'Good God!' he managed to cry, rubbing himself furiously.

When he scrambled to the bank, Flood was almost dressed. Seven turned to pick up his underwear and a powerful blow struck him painfully in the middle of the back, slamming him so hard it almost knocked him back into the stream. Catching his balance and whirling around, he saw the other man leaning on his cane, laughing at him.

'Snowball,' Flood said.

'Like t' broke my back.'

'You wouldn't want me to insult you by tossin' a fluffy little handful at you'. Flood threw the blanket to Seven. 'Dry yourself. You're goin' purple.'

During the following five weeks, while the sun's rays worked patiently at clearing the mountains, there were only two or three minor flurries of snow. Seven had a system worked out for keeping Flood a prisoner. He'd rigged a solid oak bolt on the tack room door and he never closed his eyes unless Flood was locked inside that room. Whenever he happened to be in reach of the outlaw, his hand was on his gun. He never let Flood near the lean-to where the other guns and ammunition was stored, and one day when the outlaw reached for a leather riata in the supply room, Seven pulled his gun and told him to leave it alone.

'You are right to stop me,' Flood grinned, 'because I could break your neck from thirty feet with this thing. And you're gettin' so careful you may live a while after all, but the lasso's likely to get dry rot if it ain't oiled.'

Seven oiled the riata.

In Flood's saddlebags there were two hundred ten-dollar gold pieces, two decks of cards and a small checker-board, aside from regular traveling gear. They played at cards a good deal, and Seven wound up owing Flood eighty-five dollars after two weeks of playing penny ante.

'I can't play no more,' Seven told the outlaw at that point. 'God knows how long it'll take me to get together eighty-five dollars. You'll likely by then be hung.' His last word lingered in the air for a minute like a bad odor, and

71

Seven regretted having said it, regretted that he had to take Flood back for such a purpose.

The other man tilted back in his chair and said, 'The word is hanged.'

They played for imagination stakes after that, and Seven finally owed Flood forty-eight thousand dollars, three gold mines, two saloons and eighteen women.

Then, when the snows were thinned down and firmed around them, Flood said one day, 'You're a problem, Seven. I don't exactly know what to do with you. Snow's about gone. My leg is okay. One a' these days you're goin' to decide it's time to get moving', and I ain't decided whether to go with you at all, or part way, or keep you here to play cards with – or what.'

They were finished with a game of stud, and Seven shuffled the cards thoughtfully. 'I don't figure that problem's in your hands, Flood.'

'Maybe, maybe not.' Flood shrugged and glanced at the cards. 'Mind if I cut?'

Seven put the deck down and Flood reached across the table toward it. Then, with blurring, incredible speed, his hand kept coming, balling into a fist. Seven was vaguely aware that his head was being snapped back into darkness.

With tremendous will power, he fought his way swiftly back to consciousness, and so it was that he opened his eyes as Flood was turning his back on him. Seven realized dimly that he was on the floor, that Flood had just taken his gun, and that the outlaw was confident Seven was going to be unconscious for some time. The new unused cane that Seven had cut for Flood was leaning against the wall near Seven's elbow. Gathering strength from somewhere deep within him, Seven reached for the thick branch of oak. He was swinging, even as he stood up. Flood sensed his movement and half-turned. In the following fraction of a moment Seven believed that while no normal man would have had the time, Flood could have flipped the revolver up and shot him had he not hesitated. And then the heavy club landed with a wicked thump across the outlaw's head and Flood

72

went down on his knees. Seven brought the weapon crashing down once more and Flood slumped to the side.

Taking the revolver from the other man's hand, Seven went to the supply room and cut a length of rope. He tied Flood's hands before him tightly, then stepped back.

When Flood opened his eyes a short time later he looked up, instantly alert and aware of the situation. 'By God, Seven, you've got the toughest jaw I ever saw, next to my own. You should've been out at least a couple of minutes.' He sat up, shaking his head. 'I once knocked a mule down with a punch of about that same category.'

'You coulda' shot me, couldn't you?'

Flood got to his feet. 'It's bad business to shoot a man who owes you eighty-five dollars.'

Seven went to the window and looked out at the white land streaked with brown where snow was gone. 'I was figurin' on leaving in a couple of days. But we'll go right now. We got a lot of the mornin' and the whole afternoon to travel.' He turned to Flood, his revolver in hand. 'I'll put our things together and ready the horses.'

'How long you goin' to keep me tied?' Flood worked his hands slightly. 'It ain't too comfortable.'

'Don't know. Maybe clean back to Texas.' Seven went to the door, making a wide circle around the outlaw. 'I'm in your debt by a lot more than eighty-five dollars, Flood. But I'll shoot you if I have to. Don't jump me again.'

Flood walked to the rocker and sat down. 'Do you mind if I help choose our route? There are two or three girls I'd like to say hello to along the way.'

'I'm not jokin', Flood.'

'Neither am I. It's damn near a thousand-mile trip and we might as well make the most of it.'

Seven went out to the horses.

# CHAPTER ELEVEN

When they were ready to go, Seven put Flood's coat around the outlaw and buttoned it at the neck for him, working from behind the other man. At the last minute Flood said, 'Bring that box of cigars, and light us up a couple to start the trip right.'

Seven glanced around the room. 'Anything else you wanta' take?'

'No. Guess not.'

Outside, Seven said ,'You take the bay. My roan can outrun 'er.'

In the saddle, Flood looked once more at his cabin. 'Funny, I got the damndest feelin' I'm not going to see this place again.' He turned the bay to face it squarely. 'Not that the hanging you're plannin' will ever come to pass. Because I'm dead set against it. But I still got the feelin'.'

Riding away, Flood glanced back for one last look as they rounded a bend. When his eyes came back to the trail ahead, he said, 'Just about a perfect little place. What do you think, Seven?'

'I'd say so,' Seven murmured. Then he added, 'Them ropes shouldn't cut your blood off. If they do, lemme know.'

In the middle of the fourth day they passed the place where Hennesey was buried. Seven was going to ride by but Flood saw the cross and rode over to the grave.

Neither of them spoke. They sat their horses for a minute or two and then rode on. Half an hour later Flood said, 'What you put on the marker – "He was a man." You marked him down right. One of the rarest things in the world.'

He was silent a moment. 'It was always good to have him with you – those times long gone. We'd be riding together yet, most likely, but for his notion that this world was worth taking seriously.'

74

Crossing the Colorado they moved southeast through Arizona, and on the second day beyond the big river they hit Indian signs: hoofprints of a group of six or seven unshod ponies moving in some low hills.

Flood studied the tracks, leaning over the bay's neck to look straight down into the prints made by individual hooves. 'Considerin' it ain't too cold,' he said, 'those horses couldn't have been by here more than two hours ago at most.'

Seven nodded. 'They was travelin' light, it looks like. Either a war party or huntin' party.'

Scanning the country around them, Flood said, 'Whatever else, it ain't a tea party. I'd just as soon not meet 'em with my hands tied.'

'We'll worry about that when an' if the time comes for worryin'.'

Flood lifted his tied hands and scratched his chin, his eyes roving constantly as they pushed their horses forward. 'I didn't say I was worried. I simply stated a preference.'

'You know much about tanglin' with Indians?' Seven asked from where he was riding, slightly behind the outlaw.

'Some.'

'What's your advice?'

'First off, when redskins are around, it's a sound policy to make sure everybody who can shoot a gun is armed.'

'What else?'

The other man was silent for a long time, studying the terain ahead of them and to each side. 'I got a gnawin' suspicion, Seven. We been ridin' for nearly two hours in a pretty straight line. Headin' for the pass up ahead between those two mountains, which is natural 'cause it looks to be the easiest way to go. If those braves have seen us, that pass'd be the place to wait for us.'

'You think we oughta ride up and over that low mountain half a mile south?'

'I'd say so. Nothin' to lose by it. But let's don't change directions just yet. If they are there and we switched away from the pass, they'd come after us. And have time to head

75

us off on flat land. I'd rather face 'em in rougher country, where there's things to hide behind.'

Seven felt his tension easing away as they moved closer to the pass. His eyes probing the smooth, treeless mountains to each side, he said, 'Seems there's nothin' there.'

'Don't bet on it. I swear a two-hundred-pound plains Indian and his horse can hide behind a cactus needle.'

They were less than six hundred yards from the beginning of the pass when Flood said, 'Let's veer sharp south here.'

They pulled their mounts around, breaking into an easy lope as they headed at right angles from their original direction.

Almost immediately there was a faraway, high-pitched shout from the pass and Flood yelled, 'Dig in, Seven! Let's make some speed!'

They'd raced a few yards when six Indian ponies sped out to head them off, their riders yipping shrilly. Rifles cracked sporadically from among the charging warriors, and a thin geyser of ground shot up into the air ahead of Seven's roan where a slug slammed the earth.

Seven pulled his Winchester and turned in the saddle, raising it to fire. His roan chose that second to leap a small dry-creek bed and the butt of the rifle walloped Seven painfully in the jaw as his head was jarred down. He put the carbine back and fired four shots with his revolver, and then they were lunging up the side of the low mountain. At the top of the rounded, bald mountain Seven saw Flood, head of him, pull his bay to a stamping halt. He reined his roan down.

'What the hell you stoppin' for?'

Flood nodded down the other side of the mountain. Three Indians were galloping toward it.

'Give me one Colt and we can ride through them.'

A few yards to their right, at the uppermost height of ground, there was a scattering of boulders two and three feet high.

'Ride up into there!' Seven said. 'And throw your bay down!'

Flood frowned at him and he raised his revolver.

'Hurry up!'

In the protection of the rocks, they swung down and tripped up their horses, throwing them onto the ground. Flood was several feet away from Seven. Each of the men quickly tied their horse's two front hooves together, using the reins to make swift half-hitches. Seven turned to the side where the five warriors were now rushing up the hill, snatching his Winchester as he whirled around. His first snap shot hit nothing. He gritted his teeth to force himself to calm down, and as bullets started whispering and banging on the rocks, he squeezed off his second shot. A pony on the slope below screamed and reared over backwards, pawing the air wildly. Before the pony hit the ground Seven pulled off his third round and an Indian fell from his horse, rolling loosely and brokenly over the ground. When he stopped his grotesque rolling, there was no more movement left in him. One of the remaining three riders rode by the Indian whose horse was shot and reached down to pull him up behind him. Then they raced back down the hill to get out of range.

Seven leaned forward on the rock in front of him, clenching the rifle tightly in his hands and lowering his head.

'What's the matter?' Flood yelled from his own protection. 'You hit?'

'I – I just killed a man.'

'Well, prepare to raise the score!' Flood roared. 'They're comin' at us on this other side!'

Jamming fresh cartridges into the rifle, keeping low, Seven hurried to the eastern slope and knelt behind an almost perfectly triangular flat piece of rock about eighteen inches high and a yard wide. At the foot of the slope leading away to the flatlands beyond, the three braves were charging up swiftly.

His teeth clenched hard together, Seven lined the leader up in the Winchester's sights, tracking him before he pulled the trigger. The Indian's pony had just crossed a bank of snow as the rifle cracked. The buckskin-clad rider flew backwards off the pony and did nearly a complete spinning somersault in mid-air before flopping face-down and arms-outspread in the snowbank.

The rock in front of Seven seemed to quiver slightly and he was blinded as a screeching whine filled his ears before fading into nothing. Blinking his tear-filled, smarting eyes, Seven got his sight partially back. Squinting narrowly, he could see an approaching brave aiming a rifle at Flood over his runnning pony's head. Seven pulled the trigger of his gun without bothering to aim and nothing happened. Then he remembered he hadn't levered a new cartridge into the chamber. He pumped the lever down and snapped it back and by that time the Indian had gotten to within thirty feet of Flood. Seven raised his gun and shot quickly. The Indian's rifle, pointed directly at the outlaw, boomed as Seven's bullet pounded into his side, and the slug intended for Flood went wild. The redskin managed to catch himself from going off his pony by dropping his rifle and clinging to the horse's neck. There was no time to turn the pony and the wiry little animal kept coming, charging on through the rocks around Flood with banging hooves and rushing on down the far side of the mountain.

Seven fired twice at the last Indian rushing at them. He missed both times but came close enough that the savage whirled his horse away and raced back down the slope.

As the last of the three retreated, Seven crouched and ran back to the largest rock on the western rim of the mountain. The pony that had gone through the rocks was already plunging across the flats below and, and Seven watched, the rider rolled off his back and sprawled to the ground. The pony kept going toward the plain where the Indians had finally stopped running.

Seven turned and saw Flood starting out from the rocks toward the rifle that the Indian had dropped. 'Leave it alone!' he commanded.

Flood grunted and sat down on a rock. 'You know, Seven, your damn fool stubbornness can get you killed. If they'd hit us from both sides at the same time, things would have got pretty excitin' around here.'

78

'We're both still right side up.' Seven reloaded his revolver and filled his rifle with shells. 'They got all shot to pieces, if I do say so. Maybe they'll just go away and leave us alone.'

'You did a passable job of shootin',' Flood agreed, 'even though hittin' that first fella seemed to jar you as much as him. A tough situation seems t' bring out the best in you. But they ain't goin' to go away just yet, 'cause they got some friends joinin' them from over east there.' He nodded his head toward a faraway point on the flats. Seven looked closely and at last saw a dozen points of movement two or three miles away on the wide plain.

The outlaw took a deep breath. 'You still goin' to leave me tied and without a gun?'

'Hell, Flood, I don't know what to do.' Seven wiped his face with the back of his hand. To his surprise, the hand came away bloody. 'What happened to me?'

'Your face got cut up from some flyin' rock when a slug hit the boulder in front of you. Thought you was blinded for a minute. And had that been the case, I wouldn't have been able to do much for either one of us.'

'The way you tossed that bay down and hog-tied 'er I wouldn't exactly classify you as helpless.' Seven ran his fingers over his face and traced four deep scratches. There was a tiny bit of rock still imbedded in his skin at a high place in his cheek and he scratched it out with a fingernail. He got a brace of revolvers from the roan's saddlebags, then reached down deeper for Flood's knife. He took the weapons to a point halfway between the two horses, where boulders to each side of the hill formed a broken wall of protection. Sticking the knife into the ground, he placed the guns near it. 'If you come after these guns while I'm okay, I'll take the time to shoot you. But if I'm in a bad way, hurt or dead, you can get to 'em in one jump. You can shoot all right with your wrists tied. And when you get a spare minute you can cut the ropes on this knife blade. You think that's fair enough?'

79

Flood shrugged. 'You'd be doin' yourself a favor to not get yourself shot first.'

'The thing is this. Goin' back to Texas ain't a joke to you no more. At least it's my guess that it ain't. And once you got a gun, I won't be able to take you far.'

'Maybe you got a point there.'

A slug whanged against a rock far down the slope from Flood and a moment later there was the distant sound of a shot from the approaching Indians to the east.

The outlaw stood up, stretched casually with his hands reaching out before him and then sat down behind the rock he'd been using as a chair. 'They are young, inexperienced fellas,' he said. 'Wastin' ammunition. Gettin' themselves shot up. Some trader either made a lot of money or got his scalp raised not too long ago, I'd guess. They all got good guns.'

'What kind of Indians are they?'

'Apaches, from their headbands. Don't know what tribe.'

Seven knelt behind the triangular rock and aimed his Winchester at the group of warriors just joining the single Apache who had retreated down the eastern slope.

The Indians held a brief pow-wow, sitting their ponies in a rough circle, and then started at a slow, flat-footed walk toward the mountain.

'Scare 'em a bit if you can,' Flood suggested. 'I doubt that they realize only one of us is fightin' them, and the longer they don't know it the better.'

Seven shot three rounds in rapid succession, and Flood said, 'They're still too far off. Aim about twenty feet over their heads.'

The Apaches had started to fan out from one another. Seven picked one man and fired at him twice, aiming well above his head. On the second shot the Indian's horse suddenly went down on its knees, struggled briefly to get back up, and then fell to the side. One of the Apaches raised his hand to signal the others back.

They regrouped, and after a few minutes one of them rode north toward the pass.

'What they doin'?' Seven asked.

'What they should've done in the first place – stayin' out of range and sendin' around to see what happened to the boys on the other side of the hill.' Flood glanced back at the now nearly setting sun. 'Only maybe an hour of daylight left. If they're smart they'll put off an attack until it's dark. That way they won't get picked off comin' up on us.'

Half an hour later the lone rider reached the four Apaches on the plain to the west and after talking, the five braves settled down to wait.

Seven went to the eastern slope. Their enemies to that side had disappeared and smoke began floating up in a thin stream from a shallow gulley. As Seven watched, a solitary warrior walked out of the gulley and sat down where he could watch the hilltop.

'They figure we're holed in for sure,' Flood said. 'And I guess they're right. We can't go north or south over this little range. Horse'd have to fly to get over some of those ridges and cliffs.'

Sitting down, Seven said, 'I got an idea. Tell me if it's no good for some reason.'

'Okay, shoot.'

'There ain't a horse among them Indian ponies can run with ours. Right?'

'They could keep up for a dash, but they'd fall back in the long run.'

'We can't ride through those Apaches east of us. Too many of 'em. But I'm bettin' we could run through those others. There's only four of 'em, not countin' the one afoot.'

'Count him. Five.'

'We won't be able to see them too good at night, and by the same token, they won't be able to see us too good. I say let's be ready to go down off the west slope and head back toward the pass about the time the big party is nearly on top of us. They wouldn't have no choice but to follow us over the mountain. If we can make it to the pass okay, they'll all be behind us and we go on through and come out with that whole east plain to lose 'em on.'

81

'You make it sound so damned easy I'm almost ashamed to pull such a dirty stunt on them poor Indians,' Flood said dryly.

'Anything wrong with the idea? You got a better notion?'

'It's not a bad idea. Maybe it'll work.' His hands crossed before him, Flood reached into his coat pocket for a half-smoked cigar. 'Most anything's better'n sitting here with the horrifying thought that all that's between me and a mob of bloodthirsty savages is Seven Smith. You got a light?'

Seven tossed him a small box of matches. 'Hope ya' choke on that cigar.'

Flood scratched a flame and lighted his smoke. 'I'm duly grateful for your shootin' the fella who rode damn near over my back. But this time there's about three times as many of 'em.'

Darkness came quickly when the sun went down in the western sky, and Seven found his muscles and his stomach tightening with tension as stars began to dot the sky overhead.

There was no moon. Far down in the east there was a faint glow from the fire burning out of sight in the gulley. Reading his thoughts, Flood spoke from where he was sitting to Seven's right. 'Just 'cause the fire's still there ain't no sign they are. Moon'll come up inside an hour. They'll be figurin' on having our curly heads of hair by then.'

Seven went to the other side and stared down into the darkness until his eyes ached with strain. There was a faint sound from Flood's direction and he turned, raising his rifle. 'Don't try for the Colts, Flood.'

'Just standin' up,' the outlaw said in a low voice. 'The big party's starting to move up the slope.'

Far below on the western side, Seven saw a faint shadowy movement. 'Comin' on this side too. Afoot.'

'They'll have their animals close at hand. Better get your roan untied and up.'

There was a shuddering sound from the night near Flood and Seven realized the bay was up and shaking herself. He released the roan's front legs and the mare shifted her feet.

As she brought her hind quarters up, her shoes scraped on a piece of rock and there was a shout from below.

'They know what we're doin',' Flood said. 'Let's go!'

Seven jammed the Winchester into its scabbard and, scooping up the Colts he'd put out for Flood, jumped into the saddle as the outlaw rode ahead down the western slope. He put the gun belt over his pommel and raced out after Flood.

The Apaches were yelling wildly and a fresh volley of thunder broke out as the main body of Indians stormed over the top of the mountain. Flood, riding a short distance in front of Seven, wheeled his bay slightly to the right. With an ear-splitting war whoop, he charged the horse straight at a warrior who rose up in his path. For a fraction of a second the brave couldn't decide whether to shoot or duck aside, and then it was too late to do either. The bay smashed into the man at full speed. There was a crashing thud and the Apache's limp body was thrown violently down the slope.

Beyond the point of the bone-breaking crash another shadowy figure emerged in the darkness, then another at his side. Seven concentrated on the second man, who was firing rapidly at them. At his second shot, the Indian screamed and sat down. Seven turned his attention to the Apache in front of Flood. How the outlaw had done it, Seven didn't know, but he'd somehow coaxed a fantastic spurt of speed out of the bay and was already nearly abreast of the Apache. In the dim shadows the bay plunged down at the brave. There was a crunching blow and Flood raced on. Only now he miraculously had a rifle in his tied hands. At the foot of the mountain the outlaw turned in the saddle and, holding the rifle in one hand, triggered a quick shot. Seven ducked, needlessly, for the bullet struck an Apache behind Seven who had just sprung onto his pony.

And then the two men were racing headlong across the flat towards the pass.

Flood, still far ahead of Seven, yelled 'Jesus Christ! All them repeaters, and I get me a single-shot!' He swore again and threw the rifle away.

Seven gradually drew up alongside him. 'How in hell'd you get that gun, anyhow?'

'Used tact. Asked the fella would he mind makin' me the loan of it for a time. And he said it would be his pleasure.' Flood shook his head with disgust. 'A god-damned single-shot!'

'That mountainside was sure thick with Indians.'

'Must've sent some reinforcements around through the pass as soon as it got dark.'

At the mouth of the pass they pulled their blowing horses up briefly to look behind them. The entire Apache party was thundering toward them far back in the darkness.

'Either they know they got fooled by now, or we're about to get fooled on the way through here,' Flood said.

'I'll go first.' Seven squeezed his roan ahead and galloped into the pass with a fully loaded revolver in his hand.

Five minutes later they shot out of the eastern end of the pass with a wide, free expanse of flatlands stretching before them. Seven holstered his Colt and the two men rode swiftly across the dark earth. They were two miles away from the line of mountains, and the moon was just edging up into the sky from over the horizon when the Apaches rushed out onto the flats after them.

'They aint got a chance to catch us unless one of these animals busts somethin',' Flood said. 'But with my luck, this bay's bound to trip over 'er own legs and break her neck. A single-shot!'

They rode the night through, pausing only long enough to give their mounts some vital time to walk and get rested. In gray morning light, when they could see several miles behind them and the Apaches were not in sight, Flood said, 'They've given up.'

The two men stopped, and Seven fed the horses some grain from the sack on the bay's back. Then the animals nosed idly in the snow while the men ate.

Seven said, 'What would you've done if that rifle'd been a repeater, Flood?'

The outlaw grinned. 'What would you've done if it'd been a repeater?'

'I don't rightly know.'

'Me too. All I do know is I'm damned sore it wasn't.' Flood raised his eyebrows philosophically. 'Well, that's how she goes.'

'Reachin' down at night, at a gallop, and takin' an Indian's gun away from 'im!' Seven bit off a piece of dried beef and chewed it for a while. 'You are about as lucky and strong and quick, I guess, as a fella can get.'

Flood nodded. 'I'm forced to agree on every point except the one about good luck. I'll bet that was the one and only single-shot in the bunch.'


## CHAPTER TWELVE

They traveled east and south now, and the snow became rarer, in time disappearing except on the high peaks.

'Light winter,' Flood said one sunny morning. 'Looks like spring already, and it's only mid-February.'

Twice they saw Indians from far distances, each time managing not to be seen by them, and once they passed a troop of cavalry which was in a great hurry. The officer in charge sent out a corporal to warn them against riding the Black Mesa country.

'There's reports of Apaches galore up there just now,' the corporal finished.

'You tell your boss that we just came through there, and them reports are well founded,' Flood told the soldier.

'How come you're tied?' the corporal demanded.

'Me and my friend got a bet on that I can't get untied before we get to Texas.'

'That's right,' Seven nodded. 'I gave 'im two-to-one odds.'

The corporal frowned. 'You an officer of the law?'

'Nope,' Seven told him. 'A simple gamblin' man.'

'Well, I ain't got time to find out about this.' The soldier gave them both a surly frown, then spun his horse to rejoin the cavalry command.

When he'd gone and they were headed southeast once more, Seven said, 'I can't say I know exactly what a Texas Ranger can and can't do in other states or territories. Hennesey never explained it. For all I know, arrestin' you and takin' you through all these other states is illegal.'

'May be,' Flood said. 'I ain't too up on the law myself.'

Two days later, about ten in the morning, a group of three cavalrymen rode over a hill half a mile away and spurred their horses over the sagebrush-covered land toward Seven and Flood.

Pulling to a halt a few feet from the two men, two of the soldiers wiped sweat from their faces and a heavy-set man with stripes on his jacket said, 'I'm Sergeant Cannon, Seventy-sixth Cavalry out of Fort Defiance.'

Seven nodded. 'What's your rush?'

'We got men combin' these hills for you. Who are you, and who's your prisoner?'

'Why?'

'Captain Hoenig thinks this man may be a murderer and robber who broke out of Yuma Prison last year, James Flood.' The sergeant stared at Flood with beefy distrust. 'In which case we'll escort you to the fort and relieve you of the responsibility for your prisoner.'

'Well,' Seven said, 'that ain't the case. But thanks for the offer, anyway.'

The sergeant said impatiently. 'Orders are to bring you to the Fort.' His holster flap was tucked back of his belt so that the handle of his revolver was exposed. He rested his hand on the gun butt. 'You can go back sittin' in your saddles, or tied over 'em.'

'If you be Flood, mister,' one of the others said, 'Cap Hoenig is anxious to see you. You'll like to git hung on the spot.'

'Shut up,' the sergeant ordered. To Seven, he said, 'You comin' peaceful?'

Seven whipped out his Colt as quickly as he could. The sergeant had his gun about halfway out when he was looking into the muzzle of the ranger's gun, and he dropped the revolver back into its holster. The other two soldiers looked suddenly alarmed, and one of them said, 'You'll have the whole U.S. Army down your necks!'

'Unbuckle your gun belts,' Seven said. The sergeant hesitated and he said, 'Hurry up!'

When the men had finished, Seven ordered them to strap the belts to the pommels of their McClellan saddles. As the sergeant dismounted, his hand moved close to his gun butt and Seven fired a shot over his head. The hand jerked away nervously.

'Step clear a' your horse fast,' Seven told him.

There was a movement to his side and Seven turned to see the cavalry horse near Floor lurch forward as the outlaw kicked him hard in the stomach. The soldier stepping down on the far side, his foot still in sturrip, was spilled onto the ground with a carbine in his hand. Seven told him to drop it and Flood rode a short way off to bring back the man's gelding.

'How far's it to Fort Defiance?' Seven demanded.

' 'Bout twenty-five miles,' the sergeant grumbled. 'You ain't gonna make us walk it?'

'Guess not. All I want on you is a good start.' He nodded to a tabletop mesa several miles to the east. 'That's a six, eight hour walk to the tabletop. You'll find your horses tied somewhere around it. And give your Captain Hoenig my regards. Seven Smith. Marshal out of Kansas.' He looked at the private who'd fallen, who was now dusting off his blue britches. 'Pick that rifle up and shove it back in place. Handle it awful careful.'

The cavalryman picked up the carbine, holding it by the end of the butt, and jammed it back in the saddle holster as Flood led the gelding up.

'You go ahead and lead the gelding, Flood, and I'll follow up with the others.'

They moved away from the three soldiers at a good lope. Flood's bay at one point began dropping back to that the soldier's horse was coming to a level with him. Seven called out. 'Don't you try for that carbine either, Flood!'

The outlaw turned in his saddle and grinned back. 'Ol' Seven Smith, the Kansas Tornado.'

Four hours after they'd left the cavalry horses at the mesa they stopped to look back the way they'd come. They were high on a hogsback hill and could see back twenty miles across the flatlands behind them.

'They ain't even to horse yet,' Flood said. 'Fort Defiance is no problem any more.'

'There's a lot of other forts and towns and such all along the way. I guess we got to figure every sheriff, marshal, deputy, soldier and Pinkerton man in the whole world is achin' to get his hands on you.'

'It kinds of warms your heart to know how folks want you so much,' Flood drawled.

They rode on to the east and after a time Seven said, 'Did you notice how I got the drop on that sergeant? It was a fair contest, 'cause the flap on his army holster was out of the way. I had him cold.'

'Oh, God,' Flood groaned. 'If you're goin' to start countin' cavalrymen, any six-year-old schoolboy can qualify as a top gunhand. That remark ain't worthy of you.'

'Well, dammit,' Seven muttered, 'that's the first time I been in a situation like that. And I was just statin' a fact, is all.'

'All right, Kansas Tornado – the man who outdrew a U.S. Cavalry sergeant.'

Seven started to get mad. Flood grinned at him and he felt his own deepening frown tug at the edges until he was grinning too. 'Doesn't sound too imposin', does it?' he agreed.

Since Fort Defiance was on the Arizona–New Mexico border, they knew they were well into New Mexico by the following morning, and when they started breakfast, Seven said, 'Which way you think we oughtta hit through the state, Flood?'

'I guess we're about a hundred miles from Albuquerque,' the outlaw decided. 'And that there is one place we ought not go. I got so many friends after me there that it'd take a whole army to get me through the town.'

'The feelin' must be mutual with the folks south in Socorro where you robbed that bank last year.'

Flood nodded and began to pull on his boots. 'You wouldn't care t' go back by way of Mexico City? Nobody's mad at me down there.'

Over coffee Flood said, 'I'd say head between Socorro and Albuquerque.'

'Sounds best to me.'

They rode at a southern angle to the rising sun, and over the next two days they mounted gradually through rising hills and mountains, slowly leaving behind the pinon-juniper, sagebrush and short crops of grama grass. Through country spotted with pines, aspen and fir trees they still mounted higher until at some points they reached timber line, and then their route began to go downhill once more.

'That bumpy ground we been crossin',' Flood said a week later, glancing back over his shoulder, 'is the Continental Divide, in case you didn't know it.'

'Yeah?'

'You throw a snowball off one of those high points to eastward and that snowball winds up in the Gulf of Mexico. Spit to westward and you eventually contaminate the Pacific Ocean.'

The day after they'd traversed the bleak gray-black frozen pools and streams and rocks that were the Lava Beds, they stopped in the late afternoon to let their horses drink from a small creek. Flood said that his bonds were beginning to bother him again, and Seven tied him by the neck and feet to a nearby tree, then took off the ropes so that Flood could stretch as he wished and rub his arms.

'You're gettin' to be a pretty fair jailer,' the outlaw told him. 'There ain't been more'n a dozen times in the last week that I could've made a break, and some of them it woulda been touch and go whether I'd have made it.' He sighed in the luxury of a wide stretch. 'But I do wish to hell you'd leave off them ropes on my wrists.'

'Even with 'em on,' Seven grunted, 'You're about as help-less as a goddamned mountain lion. Except for times like this, when I got complete control, they stay.'

That evening they crested a low hill in the growing dusk and saw the twinkling lights of a small town in the valley rolling away before them.

'Well, ain't that a lucky break,' Flood said. 'A nice little town poppin' up just as we're runnin' low on everything from coffee and cigars to jerky and bannock.'

'I wouldn't say you was too surprised at seein' that town,' Seven said suspiciously.

'Well, what am I supposed to do, fall off my horse with amazement?'

Seven turned back toward the distant, friendly gleam of soft kerosene lamps through the windows of the buildings below. 'We could use some supplies.'

'And it ain't a big enough place to be able to afford a regular lawman. Probably count on the law up north at Las Lunas.'

'How d'you think they'd feel about a fella ridin' through town with his hands tied? Cause a fuss? Try to hold you or me, or both of us?'

'I don't know the town any better'n you, but one thing's sure. We can't go forever without supplies.'

'Okay. Let's ride on.'

They went on down toward the cluster of frame buildings and were soon riding through the deep dust of the short, wide main street. The few people standing along the boardwalks or seated in chairs along the shadowy porches paid little attention to the two riders in the darkened street. Once, when they rode by the loungers near a well-lighted saloon, Seven thought there was a whispered stir of excitement, but nothing came of it. And then they were in front of a general store, and the pulled up to hitch their horses.

Flood's jacket was draped over his shoulders, and it was not obvious that he was bound. They walked across the plank walk before the store, their boots sounding hollowly on the wood, and entered the door. The door set a bell overhead to jangling, and a fat little man hurried out from the back of the store.

'Can I help you – well, Mr. Flood!'

'How are you, Jackson?'

'Why, I'm just fine!' the little man beamed. 'We were sure glad to hear you got out of jail!' He hesitated, glancing for the first time at Flood's hands. 'You're tied!'

'Yeah.' Flood nodded toward Seven. 'Like you to meet the man who caught me up in Utah. Name of Smith.'

Jackson turned toward Seven, his round face creased in a heavy frown. Neither of the two men spoke and Flood continued, 'We just stopped by to pick up some things we're needful of, Jackson.'

Seven told the storekeeper what they had to have, and the little man glared at him as he piled the merchandise on the counter.

There was a feminine shriek from the doorway and Seven whirled around, unconsciously grabbing the butt of his Colt. A pretty brunette with large, dark eyes stood with her arms outstretched. She was wearing a low-cut black dress, and her hair was gathered up off the back of her neck in a fancy style.

'Jim!' she shouted. 'They just told me you were here!' She rushed to Flood and threw her arms around him, drawing his face down to kiss him enthusiastically. Then she bounced away from the big man and demanded, 'Why the ropes?'

'This here is Seven Smith, Jessica. I'm his prisoner.'

The girl turned from Flood to Seven and back again. 'Why?'

'Because,' Seven explained tightly, 'he's tied an' I'm not – and I'm armed an' he's not.'

Flood picked up the box of cigars on the counter and banged it so that the top came open. He took one of the smokes out and the storekeeper quickly struck a match to give him a light. The outlaw said, 'This fella may look like a pleasant, easy-goin' young man, but when he gets rollin', Jessica, he's hell on wheels.'

Another girl came into the store and hurried over to Flood. 'Jim,' she said happily, 'where the devil have you been keepin' yourself?'

Seven put the money on the counter for their purchases. 'So you don't know anybody in this town, don't know nothin' about the town – huh, Flood?'

'Well, I have been here a couple of times before,' the outlaw admitted. 'And there's some folks here who know me.'

'Some?' the new girl said. 'Everybody in town. There isn't a person who doesn't love you or else want to shoot you.'

Seven picked up his change. 'Put all that stuff in a gunny sack, mister,' he told the storekeeper. When this was done, Seven tossed the sack over his shoulder and said, 'If you can tear yourself away from these friends of yours, Flood, we're leavin'.'

'He's got to come over to the Chrysolite and have a few drinks with us,' Jessica said indignantly, and the other girl pouted, 'We've not seen Jim in two years!'

'Go ahead, Flood.' Seven stepped aside to let the outlaw walk out first.

In the street the girls and Flood talked and laughed together while Seven tied the sack onto the bay's back. As he finished the work and stepped back, one of the girls shouted down the street toward the well-lighted saloon:

'Hey, in the Chrysolite! Come help us get Jim Flood to take a drink.'

The saloon started erupting with people.

'Let's get goin'!' Seven told Flood.

'I'm willin' to try, but I'd doubt we'll make it.' Flood stepped to the bay and Seven hurried to his roan. The outlaw seemed to be having some difficulty getting his foot in the stirrup, and Seven found his right leg gripped firmly at the ankle as he started to swing up. Turning, he saw the second girl holding him.

'Let go a' my leg, ma'am,' he said.

'My name's Millie. Don't be in such a hurry.'

And then a swarm of happy, shouting men and women from the saloon surrounded them in a sea of shouts and laughter. Seven tried unsuccessfully to mount his roan. He lost sight of Flood briefly as the man was shoved in the direction of the Chrysolite.

Seven pulled his Colt, aimed it at the sky and triggered three roaring blasts. There was a moment of relative silence as the curious merrymakers turned toward him.

'Flood can go and do some drinkin' with you,' Seven shouted, 'but I'm stayin' next to 'im, and there's goin' to be some goddamned order about it!' He pushed a man away and made his way toward Flood. Standing at his side, he said, 'Okay, let's go, and keep it peaceful!'

The crowd roared along the street toward the saloon as soon as Seven stopped talking. Both he and Flood were swept into the swinging doors of the Chrysolite in a wave of celebration-bound human beings, most of whom still did not know Flood was tied and unarmed.

Room was made at a big table near the wall and soon a dozen people were sitting around the table with three times that number standing around it in a deep circle.

'Where ya' been keepin' yourself?' a man called from across the table.

'What's your score these days? Pushin' thirty ain't it?' another called waving a glass of beer.

'Why in hell,' a girl with several chins and a big, bouncy bosom asked, 'did you only shoot three of them men in the Socorro First National last year?'

Flood, with Millie and Jessica sitting to his left and right, and a blonde girl hugging him from behind, did not bother answering any questions. 'Is Yoder still playin' piano here?' He lifted a glass of whiskey and at least five people asked with indignation or laughter why he was tied. 'Get ol' Yoder to bang out some tunes!'

In a moment loud, gay piano music started from across the room.

'That's the boy!' Flood shouted. He turned to Jessica. 'Yoder remembers I like *The Utah Trail*.'

Millie, sitting –between Seven and Flood, jabbed the Ranger with her elbow. 'You're not drinkin', honey,' she told him. 'No point stayin' sober.'

There was a shot of whiskey before Seven, and as he glanced at it, the barman leaned over and put down a second one.

'Who's buyin' all this liquor?' Seven asked her.

'Everybody, honey. They're fightin' for the privilege, and Sam's insistin' every second round's on the house. Drink up!'

After his fourth drink, Seven realized the situation was out of his control. Millie hugged him and said, 'What you thinkin' about, handsome?'

'I can't beat this fuss down, so I'll jus' have to let 'er buck it out.'

She giggled. 'Say, how come a lawman and Jim ever got to be friends?'

In the general noise, shouting and laughter, Seven didn't hear her question, and when she repeated it, he said, 'What makes you think we're friends?'

'Well, Sam just asked Jim a minute ago if he wanted your head busted, and Jim said no, thanks.'

Seven turned around and saw there was a space between him and the wall for a man to get behind him. He shifted his chair back flush with the wall.

'How you doin'?' Flood asked, leaning across in front of Millie. 'Ain't this a friendly town?'

'Sure is,' Seven agreed.

After an hour of heavy drinking the crowd around the table had thinned down somewhat. Flood was concentrating most of his attention on Jessica, and Millie was trying to make conversation with Seven, when Seven noticed a sudden, growing quiet in the room. Flood had just finished a drink and his hands were under the table. He looked up and Seven followed his gaze. Moving to lean against the bar several feet away was a tall, skinny man with an uneven beard and dirty clothes that hung loosely from his frame. The only thing neat about him was the matching set of smooth-worn walnut-handled revolvers hanging from his hips on twin gun belts.

The people between him and Flood moved back out of line as he said, 'What's the bounty on your head these days, Flood?'

Flood smiled at him. 'Haven't counted it of late, Graves. Enough to buy a one-way ticket to everlastin' hellfire, that's for sure.'

'I've had an itch to collect it.'

Flood leaned back slightly in his chair. 'I'll bet you've got all kinds of itches.'

'Not in my place, you won't collect no reward on Jim Flood,' the man behind the bar said.

Graves inched back along the curved bar so that his back was to the wall and he could watch the barman out of the corner of his eye. 'This your argument, Sam?'

Buffaloed, the other man muttered, 'Maybe not.'

Graves turned his attention to Flood. 'Bounty collector's gotta make a livin' too. Heard you was tied, Flood, but don't quite believe it.'

'You damned well know his hands are tied,' Jessica told him, 'or you wouldn't even be in town!'

Graves said, 'I figure you be a mortal like the rest, Flood. Bullets'll kill ya', and that's what I'm here for.' He glanced with hard eyes at the people grouped in the saloon. 'Ain't nobody here'll try t' stop me.'

'Mister,' Seven said quietly, 'you're stopped.'

Graves studied him, his gaze stern and calculating, then dismissed him. 'Keep out, kid.'

'I'm already in. I got a forty-five under this table pointin' about where your belt buckle is. You lift a hand to hurt Flood, you'll get blown clean through that wall.'

'You a New Mexico lawman?' Graves demanded. 'Duly swore?'

'Depends on how you look at it.'

'You won't get no reward for 'im. He's worth somethin'

more than ten thousand dollars, if you let me take 'im in. We could settle it later between us.' The bearded man paused. ' 'Less you're from outta state. An' got no papers on 'im. Then I can take 'im away from ya'.'

'Try.'

Graves' face twisted in uncertainty, but the greediness in his eyes was strong enough to make his hand stab toward the gun on his right hip.

The table bounced slightly and there was a muffled roar from under it that echoed boomingly from the rafters above. Seven leaped away from the girls and Flood to draw Graves' fire if he had missed, and Flood shoved Jessica's chair away from him so that the girl was away from the line of shooting.

Graves was thrown back with savage force against the wall. He had his gun in his hand, but he'd had no time to cock it and it was thrown from his hand by the jarring slug from Seven's gun. On the floor, he reached for his other revolver, then thought better of it and lay moaning with pain.

Seven crossed to the fallen man and took his second gun. The barman knelt to look at Graves' wound and glanced up over his shoulder at Seven. 'Just busted his leg high up. Missed his belt buckle a foot.'

Flood was beside Seven then, and he said, 'This Smith is a charitable fella, Sam. He coulda' hit Graves in the middle if he'd wanted.'

'Is there anybody to patch him up?' Seven asked.

'Yeah.' Sam took off his apron. 'I'll go get the blacksmith.'

Half an hour later the party was in full swing again. Seven took two more shots to settle his stomach from jumping around. Then he knew he was a little high and he quit. Flood was drinking at a fantastic rate. Around midnight he whispered to Seven,

'Jailer, could you find it in your heart to give me some time off for good behaviour?'

'Huh?'

96

'Jessica and me are old friends and we can't do any friendly visitin' with this gang around.'

'Every girl in the place seems to be an old friend of yours.'

'Jessica's special. She's got a nice, cozy room up at the head of those stairs. We'd like to go up there and talk about old times.'

'Talk about old times?'

Flood nodded. 'Old times.'

'Then we go?'

'Right.'

'Okay. Just a minute.' Seven left Flood sitting in his chair and went up the stairs. Standing where he could watch the outlaw, Seven opened the door and looked in. Then he waved Flood up. When they were both in the room, Seven looked out the small window and saw that it was too far down to jump. He searched the few pieces of furniture in the room for weapons and found none. Then he went over Flood, feeling the man's pockets from behind. 'They coulda' give you everythin' but a Gatling Gun by now,' he muttered thickly.

There was no weapon on Flood and as Seven turned to go out, Jesica came to the door. The thought that she might have a gun occurred to Seven. He stared at the girl's slender body under the thin dress, realized he was staring and blushed awkwardly. She smiled at him and he went to the door. For some reason he felt it necessary to say something, if only to cover up for his embarrassment.

He said, 'Well, here's to old times.' Immediately twice as uncomfortable, he shut the door behind him and went back down to the main floor of the saloon.

At the table, Millie put her arms around his right arm in a kittenish gesture of affection. 'I just love strong men!'

'Ma'am?'

'They'll be up there a while. Let's you and me have a high ol' time too!' She snuggled closer to him. 'I got a room next door.'

'I gotta stay and keep an eye for Flood.'

'Oh, come on!' She purred the invitation and Seven noticed to his dismay that Millie was much prettier than he'd originally noticed.

'To be honest, the idea appeals to me. But dammit, Millie, Flood's my prisoner.'

'He could've told Sam to bust your head for him.'

'True.'

'If Jim Flood is anybody's prisoner, he's just doing it to be polite.' She hugged him and, leaning close, bit his ear. 'Come on!'

'All right, goddamnit!'

When Jim Flood came downstairs, alone, it was nearly two o'clock in the morning and there were only a few people still in the saloon. Seven was half-dozing at the table with his arm around Millie, whose head was resting on his chest.

Seven saw Flood and leaned forward. Millie raised her head as his weight shifted. She smiled and said, 'Jim, bring him back with you soon. He is one of the sweetest men in the world.'

Flood chuckled. 'He is a darlin', all right.'

Seven glowered at empty space before him. 'You ready to go?'

'Uh-huh.'

Standing up, Seven took off his hat and said, 'It's been nice knowin' you, Miss Millie.' He twisted the brim of his hat nervously and added, 'I won't never forget you.'

She stood up and smiled. 'No. I don't think you will.'

Outside, where lamplight streamed through one of the Chrysolite windows, Seven stopped Flood to check the ropes on his wrists. 'These ain't my knots.'

'No. But Jessica put 'em back just about the way they was before. I told her the whole thing was kind of a game, which applyin' to anything in life ain't far from wrong.'

The storekeeper, Jackson, was sitting on a rocker in front of his general store. He said, 'I fed and watered your animals, Mr. Flood.'

'Obliged.'

They rode out of town and as the lights dimmed in the darkness behind them, Seven said, 'Jesus, I really went haywire tonight.'

'I don't know. I've seen wire off of bales of hay that seemed more twisted up.'

'I forgot all about the horses.'

'That happens.'

'And there was that girl, Millie.'

'Hell, Seven, a man without some stallion in him ain't worth a damn to a man or woman.'

'And there was Graves.'

'I was sort of pleased with the way you handled him.'

'Why?'

Flood turned his head and looked at Seven in the deep shadows. 'What was your impression of that fella?'

'Dirty. Unpleasant bastard. But his guns had a well-used look about 'em, and he wore them comfortable. That's it. There was a chance, it seemed to me, that he could get his weapons out faster'n me.'

Flood grinned. 'There was a chance, all right. Graves is one of the best gunfighters in New Mexico. If you'd tried him head on, we'd be thinkin' up a marker for your headpiece right now. Probably somethin' like "He Won Second Place, Fair and Square".'

'They'd be diggin' a hole big enough for the two of us, I guess.'

'That's right except you forget – I'm never going to die. Life is too much fun for me to let that happen.' Flood was silent for a moment, and then he said, 'The thing I'm most curious to know is, where the hell were you tryin' to hit Graves?'

'You probably won't believe me. High up in the leg. Thought it'd knock him down and take the fight out of 'im.'

# CHAPTER THIRTEEN

They crossed the southern tip of the Manzano Mountains and moved on across the Chupodera Mesa into Lincoln County. Seven made it a point to avoid the few villages and settlements along the way. Just once, at the eastern edge of Lincoln County, they stopped at a lonely trading post to buy grease and salt and a few pounds of beans.

There were some Albuquerque newspapers for sale at the post and they were only a few days old, so Seven bought three of them that stretched over the first, second and fourth of March.

They made camp early that night and read the papers before supper.

Flood took the second of March and Seven took the first and fourth.

'I'll be damned,' Seven said after a few minutes.

'What?'

'Says here a wellknown bounty hunter, name of Fred Graves, was found dead in Valencia County. Shot twice, once in the leg, and once in the head.' Seven handed the paper to Flood.

Flood read the brief account on the back page and laughed. 'You put a man like him out of commission and sometimes he don't last long. He's got a lot of enemies in some circles.' Flood corrected himself, 'Or he had enemies, rather.'

'In a way,' Seven said quietly, 'I killed him.'

'You sad about it?'

'No, I guess not, actually.' Seven took his hat off and scratched his head. 'It's just too bad there has to be so much killin' going on.'

Flood shrugged. 'Hell, don't worry about it. People have been dyin' for years. Being strong enough to kill is just half of it. You also got to be strong enough to forget about it –

or you're killin' yourself at the same time.' He grinned at Seven. 'You remember what I say. It's important in your line of work. Like Lot's wife. She was weak and she looked back and she turned into a pile of salt. That's one of the rare intelligent things in the Bible. You can't look back.'

'But you can't help looking back,' Seven argued. 'At least most people can't.'

'I'm not talking to most people. I'm talking to you. Let the others look back. I think you got the strength to forget what's best forgot.'

Seven got up and started to make supper. Cooking beans over the fire later, he said, 'I'm surprised you didn't have books in your cabin in Utah. I'd peg you as a sort of readin' type fella.'

Flood looked up from the papers he was still going through. 'I used to read as a boy. But on the face of it, books and book-learnin' is for second-raters. A real first-class man lives hard and fast, rather than readin' about life – and what else is there to read about? He does his own thinkin', rather than finding out what other people have thought.' He folded the paper. 'You got to put more salt in them beans. At least one more good pinch.'

They were moving down the Pecos two days later, looking for a likely spot to cross, when Seven's roan stepped on a smooth rock and slipped. She landed on one knee and whinnied in pain, rolling onto her side. Seven jumped out of the stirrup as she rolled over.

Flood, a few feet in front, reined the bay up and got down. 'She broken or just banged up?'

'Don't know,' Seven said. He held the roan's head and tried to quiet her. 'Easy, girl. Whoa, now.'

Flood came up and looked at her thrashing forelegs. 'They don't usually go down that way unless a leg's gone.'

'I know,' Seven murmured. 'I think she busted her knee.' He added fiercely to keep the growing edge out of his voice, 'Goddammit! She goes through some of the meanest country in the world full gallop! She ducks Indian arrows and bullets! And walkin' nice and easy, this has to happen to 'er!'

The mare's forelegs stopped their wild movements for a moment, and Flood put his hand on the knee that was starting to bleed a little. 'It's gone.' He stepped back as she lashed out again and then lay still.

Flood walked to the bay and stood beside her, looking out over the Pecos.

Seven felt as if there were glue in his throat. He took the mare's bridle off, talking gently to her as he unbuckled the chinstrap and slipped out the bit. As he took his gun out, the thought came to him that the roan had seen guns used a good deal. Could she possibly have an idea what guns were for? He came up from behind her so that she could not see the revolver, and a moment later a shot echoed out across the river.

Joining Flood near the bay, Seven said, 'I liked the way you left your saddle on that pinto of yours. But – dammit, I can't afford that kind of thing! I gotta get all that gear off her, the saddle included!'

Flood turned around, his lean face softened with understanding. Hell, yes. It's a different situation, altogether. I think there's a settlement about two miles down river. We can walk it.'

They reached the settlement, a group of ten or twelve buildings, about noon. It was a stopover for freighters, and the one large stable was at the end of town they entered. Seven was lugging his Winchester and had his saddlebags thrown over his shoulder, and Flood was leading the bay. They stopped at a big open door and Seven called in, 'Anybody there?'

The stable door at the far end of the building banged shut and a thin, bald little man with a blacksmith's apron came out to the street.

'Want to buy a horse,' Seven said.

'I own some,' the man said. 'Out back. Come on. Got thirty, forty good mules. You wouldn't ruther have a mule?'

'No. A horse.'

'Got six or eight. Couple of nice ones.'

There were corals at the back of the big barn, and the

102

little man pointed out six horses all together in one fenced area. 'That's the lot. All mares and geldings.'

They stood silently for a few minutes, looking at the animals.

'Strawberry roan ain't a bad bit a' horseflesh,' the little man said at last. 'Give ya' a good price on 'er.'

'Too heavy-headed. Too big hooves. She's more a work horse than I'm after,' Seven told him. 'What you think?' he asked Flood.

'Got to be the blazed black or the gray. I'd say the black.'

'Uh-huh. You wanna get that black out here, Mister?'

'Good mare,' the man said. 'Only five years old. Sound as a dollar.'

Seven bought the black mare for eighty-five dollars and as the stable owner was making out a bill of sale, he looked up at the two tall men and said, 'Take it you lost a horse.'

'Yeah,' Seven said.

'You wanna rest up from your walk, I got a boy who can ride out bareback and get your stuff and put it on the black.'

'I'd be much obliged, mister.'

Seven told the man where his roan was and the man said, 'There's a bar down the street where you can wait.'

Before they started down the street Flood said, 'You are the first fella I can recall who ain't asked me why my hands are tied. Obliged for that, too.'

The man bit off a chew of Star Tobacco and put the plug back in his pocket. 'Its none a' my business.' He called over his shoulder as he started back into the barn, 'My boy'll tie the black next to your bay.'

At the bar there were two bulky mule skinners arguing about the best route between Portales and Carrizozo and behind the counter was a bearded, surly barman.

Both Seven and Flood ordered whiskey and the man stared at them in sullen silence for a moment, then said, 'Ain't sure I wanna serve no tied man in my place.' He shook his head. 'Ain't sure at all.'

Seven said flatly, 'I am sure enough for two of us, Mister.'

The barman tried to stare down Seven, failed and turned to get glasses.

One of the mule skinners called in a jeering voice, 'Whatcha' got there, young fella, a horse thief?'

Seven turned toward the man angrily, but before he could speak the other skinner said loudly, 'Jesus God Almighty! That there is Jim Flood! I seen 'im once up to Santa Fe. Holy Jesus!' He finished his drink at one throaty gulp and started for the door. 'I gotta go tell ol' Barnes! He oughtn't miss no chance t' see Jim Flood!'

The first muleskinner glanced again at Flood's bound hands as his friend hurried out the door. 'You're Flood?' He hooked his thumbs around the straps of his dirty coveralls and spit accurately at a brass spittoon near his feet. 'You don't look like much t' me.'

Within a few minutes a brawny, ragged bunch of freighting men began wandering into the bar. They gathered in small groups of three or four and stared at Flood, muttering among themselves and drinking only as a sideline.

'You sure as God Jim Flood?' a black-bearded giant demanded from halfway down the bar.

Flood nodded. 'Sure as God.'

'Can't see what's t' be scared of 'bout you.'

'Me neither, Blacky,' a short, barrel-chested man said from across the room near a pot-belly stove. 'You be able t' whup 'im one-handed!'

'Bet you'd even b'able t' whup 'im, Shorty!' someone said from a group near the door, and the men in the room laughed coarsely.

Flood said, 'Go another round, Seven?'

'Yeah.' Seven motioned to the bartender.

Filling their glasses, the barman said with a lip-curling snicker, 'Don't mind the boys. They's a tough bunch is all, and they ain't scared to speak out their mind.'

'That's okay,' Flood said. 'Fellas working with mules all the time are bound to have some jackass rub off on them.'

The freighters were getting louder in their talk, and none

104

of them heard what Flood said. The barman frowned and took the money Seven put on the counter.

The room kept filling and the crowd became louder, bolder, more insistent upon insulting Flood. Seven, his back to the wall at the end of the bar, kept watching for the black mare, but he could see through the dirty front window that the bay stood alone. He kept an eye on the door and was grateful that at least the men who came in were unarmed.

A sandy-haired man wearing only his red underwear above his pants tossed off a drink near Flood and turned toward the outlaw. 'You take a gunman's guns away from 'im and what've you got?' he demanded.

'You got his guns,' Flood answered softly.

The sandy-haired man's forehead creased with slow thought and then anger. He slammed his glass down on the bar. 'I didn't ask for no smart answer!'

'Nobody asked you for a stupid question.'

There was a wave of movement farther down the bar and Blacky bellowed, 'What you say, Dick?'

The bartender leaned over the bar and spoke to him.

'What?' the giant roared. 'Boys, that suck-egg mule at the end of the bar says we's all jackasses!' He waded through the crowd toward Seven and Flood with men falling in behind him. 'Let's see what the yella-bellied bastard says to my face!'

'Wait a minute, Blacky!' someone yelled from near the window. 'Here comes Deputy Lovell!'

Seven pulled a Colt as Blacky and the freighters came on toward him and Flood. 'Stop where you are,' he said.

Something nudged him in the back and he turned to see the barman holding an old Sharp's buffalo gun on him.

'Put the gun back,' the barman said nervously.

Flood glanced at Seven. 'Do it.'

Seven holstered the Colt and a voice called from the door. 'What's goin' on here?'

'Come in, Lovell!' Blacky called over his shoulder. 'We got us a badman here!'

An overweight red-faced man with a revolver in his hand

pushed through the circle of men until he stood before Seven and Flood. 'What's goin' on, Blacky?'

'This here's the great Jim Flood, the yella-bellied bastard. I'm about t' break 'im up some.'

Lovell waved his gun uncertainly between the two men. 'I'm a deputy sheriff,' he said, the words stuttering over each other. 'And – and I better find out—'

'Find out hell!' someone shouted. 'Let Blacky beat the bastard up! He killed a friend a' mine in Tijeras!'

'Why not hang 'im?' another cried, and twenty men yelled in spontaneous agreement.

Seven saw the barman put down his Sharp's now that the deputy had his gun pointed at them. The sandy-haired man said, 'You wouldn't try stoppin' me an' Blacky and the boys from lynchin' such a murd'rous hombre, would ya'?'

Lovell seemed to shrink under the stares of the bigger men around him, and he said, 'I coulda' rode into town ten minutes later, I guess.'

'First I'm agoin' t' smash 'im a couple of times!' Blacky decided.

Seven knew instinctively what Flood was going to do. And he reached for his gun at the instant the outlaw's foot lashed out and kicked Lovell's gun out of his hand.

'Don't move closer,' Seven told Blacky. 'And, barman, keep clear of your rifle.'

'He can't hold off all of us!' someone growled from the rear of the circle of men. 'Let's take 'em!'

Seven noticed through the window that the black mare had now been hitched next to the bay outside. 'Flood,' he said.

The outlaw seemed to know what Seven was thinking too. He turned quickly, his hands stretched toward the ranger, as Seven raised his knife and cut the ropes binding his wrists.

'Get 'em!' a man insisted. 'They's only two!'

Seven fired over the heads of the men pushing closer. 'Clear the way!'

The freighters moving up from the rear kept shoving, and Blacky threw out his huge hands to grab Flood. The outlaw ducked under the giant's arms and his right fist disappeared in a blurring arc as he hit Blacky in the abdomen. The big black-bearded man grunted explosively and was thrown back and down as though he'd been kicked by a horse. Bringing his fist back in a second invisible curve of swift motion, Flood backhanded the sandy-haired man at the bar with such furious force that the man was lifted up and over the bar and knocked the bartender down as he crashed over the counter.

Flood turned to Seven with a faint grin turning into a smile as the joy of battle caught him. Come on! We'll clear a path!'

The deputy, Lovell, bent down near Seven and tried to scoop his gun up off the floor. Seven brought his Colt barrel down on Lovell's head and the lawman dropped flat on his face. A flying fist knocked Seven back against the wall, and with his shoulders still against the wall, Seven brought up a foot and booted the man who owned the fist away from him.

Flood was halfway across the room now, roaring with sheer enjoyment and surging against a solid wall of husky freighters before him. Seven dropped his gun into its holster again and started for Flood. A man on the floor tripped him and Seven went down, twisting neatly to land with his knee in the man's stomach. As the Ranger struggled back up, Flood sent a man flying off balance across the room where he slammed into the pot-belly stove and the stove and various lengths of stovepipe went banging to the floor, sending up thick clouds of black and gray soot.

A man jumped Flood from behind and Seven grabbed him by the throat, strangling him as he pulled him off the outlaw. The man squirmed around in Seven's grip and hit him in the face. He tried to kick Seven in the groin, but Seven moved, taking the speeding boot on the leg instead. Then Seven's long, looping left caught the man between the eyes and sent him down in the middle of the floor.

Flood was almost to the door now, and Seven had a glimpse of men running away out on the street. A lanky skinner picked up a chair and swung it wildly at Flood. The outlaw ducked and the weight of the man's own swinging momentum took both him and chair on around and through the wide window at his side.

Somebody slugged Seven behind the ear as he came up even with Flood and Seven struck blindly back, feeling someone's nose crunching under his knuckles. Something banged down on Seven's head. He saw shooting sparks of various colored lights in a surrounding sea of darkness for a moment, and his ears began to ring as his sight came back. Flood was at the door and with one last powerful blow he knocked a wide, bearish-looking opponent out the door and down the steps beyond.

'Let's go!' Seven yelled, realizing he was talking too loudly because of the ringing in his ears. He ran to the black mare and unhitched her. The bearish muleskinner on the street got up and lumbered toward Flood, and the outlaw flattened him with a walloping right that lifted the man's heels off the ground.

A rifle boomed from down the street as Flood dashed to the bay and leaped into the saddle. He reached down under her neck and snapped the leather reins with one hand, leaving neat leather strips hitched to the rail and attached to nothing. The two men wheeled their horses swiftly and raced out of town as still other big guns began to crash and boom behind them.

Deputy Lovell stumbled onto the street and called, 'You men can be my posse! Let's go after 'em!'

At a wide sandy spot in the river, Seven and Flood galloped across to the eastern side, and three minutes later a posse of fifteen men on mules and horses thundered across the river in wild sprays of flying water to rush after the disappearing men.

Looking back, Flood said, 'They ride like mule skinners. They couldn't catch us in a year.'

Seven's legs felt strange pressing down around the black. She was thinner than the roan had been, and there wasn't as much to hold onto, nor was she as comfortable to sit. But she had more than enough pep, and she was sure-footed as a deer. Seven glanced back. 'I got a hunch they ain't too eager to catch up to you, Flood. Way you cleaned a path through that room! There was near two dozen fellas in there!'

'Most of the fightin' was done when the black-bearded gent got himself whopped. In any crowd more fellas are anxious to watch than to take part.' Flood suddenly yelled a long, high blasting whoop that exploded at the end in a deafening 'Yow!' He took off his hat and swatted the bay on the fanny. 'Nothin' like a good knuckle fight t' get a man's blood runnin'! You didn't do bad yourself, Seven!'

Seven wiped his hand across a split in his lip and the fingers came away wet and red. 'Well, I got my blood runnin',' he said, 'in three or four places.'


CHAPTER FOURTEEN


By mid-afternoon the pursuing men had given up the chase, and when Seven and Flood halted a few miles farther east Seven retied the outlaw and they continued traveling as before, heading straight out through the Staked Plains country.

Three days later, about nine in the morning, Flood took a deep breath as they rode over a small hill where tall wild grass was waving lazily in a warm wind. 'This smells like Texas to me.'

'You think we're over the border?'

'Yep.' Flood nodded at some jutting hills in the distance whose rolling lesser foothills descended in gradual waves to where the men were. 'The Mustang River ain't far from them little sawtooths.'

That afternoon a man on a big gray with black mane and tail appeared on a ridge more than a mile away. He sat his horse idly, as though he were vaguely curious, then turned and rode out of sight.

'Rancher, you think?' Seven asked Flood.

'Maybe,' Flood frowned. 'Maybe. Not too common a color horse, that gray with black markings.'

'No, it isn't.' Seven was mildly discomfited for some reason. 'We can swing a little deeper south toward the Devil.'

'Might be a good idea.'

That night they camped at a small tributary of The Mustang. Seven started to gather wood for a fire and Flood said, 'I wouldn't cook tonight.'

'Just a hunch,' Seven asked, 'or somethin' definite?'

'A hunch.'

They ate their cold jerked beef and bannock in thoughtful silence. Later, Seven said, 'That fella a friend of yours?'

'He could be a man I knew. Had a horse like that.'

In the morning they struck camp and moved on toward the Devil River. Just before straight-up noon they stopped to let their horses drink at a winding creek, and Flood laughed. 'Say, you know what we oughtta do? We oughtta think of some good reason to go into Odessa. I got some friends there you'd get a kick out of.'

'Lucinda?'

'That's one of 'em. How'd you know?'

'When we followed you through there last year, she said t' tell you she'd marry you.'

'I'll be damned. An' here I thought the girl liked me.' Flood got down and scooped himself a drink, twisting his wrists so he could dip water in his right palm. Back on the bay he said, 'You're plannin' on marryin' that girl named Harrington?'

Seven pulled the black's head up. 'I'd like t' try, unless she's said all right to some other fella while I been galavantin' around the country after you.'

Deeper in the afternoon, when valleys were filling blue with shadows from the hills, Seven saw a flash of movement far away on a crest to their right. He looked up in time to see a rider on a pinto with a solid black head and chest walk into sight and then, briefly, behind the first horse there appeared the gray with black mane and tail. Then both horse-men disappeared back over the edge of the crest.

'See 'em?' he asked Flood.

'Yeah. It was Ennis on the gray. Thought it might be him before. Man on the pinto'll be Parkman. And I'd guess Burns and Ritter won't be far off.'

'Who are they?'

'You got t' stop askin' questions sometimes,' Flood laughed without much humor, 'because some of the questions you put mark you as unbelievably ignorant. They are a group of fellas who do things that are usually against the law. One of their favored pastimes is robbin' trains. And they're also known for being among the top-grade gun-fighters in the southwest. All four of 'em.'

'What they interested in us for?' Seven pulled out his Winchester and held it across the pommel of his saddle, studying the ridge where the men had disappeared.

'Their interest is in me. Couple of years ago they went to the trouble and time and effort of robbin' a train. And then I robbed them of the money they'd robbed. They are about six-thousand-dollars worth sore at me.'

'How could they've found us?'

'Anybody's guess.'

'Let's circle off to the left here.'

They angled east at a lope, away from the ridge. After forty minutes they dropped to a walk as they started through a canyon with steep walls to each side of them. Flood's eyes moved rapidly along each edge of the canyon, swiftly check-ing off each detail. Turning to Seven, who was slightly be-hind him and still holding the Winchester in his hand, he said,

'I don't like this setup. I'd like you to give me a gun. If those fellas come down on us, there mayn't be time to talk much.'

'I'm willin' to get myself shot to keep them from gettin' you, Flood. But I can't give you a gun.'

'Untie me and give me a gun, Goddammit,' Flood told

111

him. 'You underestimate these boys and it'll be your last estimate.'

'We made it all the way from Utah so far okay.'

'We've not come up against anythin' quite like this!'

The mouth of the canyon was only a hundred yards away when two riders appeared suddenly behind a wall of rock. Completely silent, and with deadly certainty in their actions, they walked their horses to the center of the canyon and waited motionlessly as Seven and Flood rode forward.

'That's Burns and Ritter,' Flood said quietly to Seven.

'Can we run?'

'Uh-uh. Other two'll be comin' up the canyon behind us by now. These fellas are too sure a' themselves.'

Seven squeezed his black imperceptibly so that she caught up with and passed the walking bay, putting Seven between Flood and the two silently waiting men. As they drew closer the Ranger could see that the men each had leathery, stern faces with agate-hard eyes. One of them had a torn, ragged scar continuing from the edge of his lips as though his mouth had been ripped open from the inside.

Near them, Seven pulled to a halt, his Winchester casually pointed at the men.

'You fellas are blockin' our path,' he said.

The man with the scar spoke, his lips hardly moving. 'Who's he, Flood?'

'Nobody you'd be interested in, Burns. Your business is with me.'

Burns nodded, his head moving forward very slightly just once. 'Got you all tied up for us, like a birthday present.'

The other man showed almost black teeth in a thin smile. 'Coulda' picked you off from ambush. But that wouldn't been so much pleasure.'

Seven heard from behind them the striking of horses' hooves over rock and knew that the other two men were closing in rapidly. 'One thing you don't know,' he said. 'This rifle don't have to be levered. I been ridin' with it cocked. Which one of you thinks he can get his gun out before I pull the trigger?'

112

The man with black teeth, Ritter, said, 'You're bluffin'.'

'If you ain't,' Burns added in a whisper, 'you'll be dead before you can get off a second shot. Why don't you ride on by yourself? We don't want you.'

Seven was aware that Flood's bay had moved up near him. Seven said, 'We're both ridin' through.'

Ritter's hand streaked toward his gun and Seven swung the Winchester's barrel half an inch and pulled the trigger. The rifle roared, lifting Ritter off his horse. Then Seven was hit twice at almost the same moment, as something at his side slammed hard against him and threw him to the ground.

Lying on his back, Seven saw the black mare rear high above him. She came down with hooves that would have crushed the life out of him if they'd struck, but she almost fell over, twisting to the side as she descended, in order not to hurt him. He had a vague sensation of feeling grateful, and at the same time wondered at the fact that Flood seemed to be the only living thing moving swiftly. His mare and Ritter's horse were moving slowly. Burns was swinging his revolver toward Flood in an absurdly slow motion. Flood had a revolver in his right hand. He lifted both tied hands together to fire over the bay's neck, and Burns never finished swinging his gun. His hand dropped and he shot his own horse in the withers, which seemed to Seven a completely absurd thing to do. The animal shrilled in pain as the slug tore into her and she turned and raced away. Ritter raised himself very slowly and Flood had all the time in the world to recock his revolver, turn around in the saddle as the bay whirled in panic, and shoot Ritter in the forehead before the man could pull the trigger of his gun.

Then, moving with ludicrous slowness, the riders on the gray and the paint came up the valley. The galloping horses stopped short as the men hauled back on the reins. Both of them began to shoot but it was dragged-out, wasted effort. One of them who looked like a Mexican was flung out of the saddle as two bullets crashed into his chest. The other man raced his horse away. Flood's gun roared once more and the man's back jerked as though hit with a heavy hammer. Dust flew from his coat and he slumped forward. But he stayed with the horse and disappeared around a bend below.

Flood watched the retreating man go, and Seven's mind gradually came out of the haze in which everything had seemed to happen so slowly. He raised himself and, sitting up, could see that his jacket was covered with blood. He could feel a warm liquid running down his cheek too, and he knew he'd been hit somewhere in the head.

Flood at last threw the gun in his hand to the ground. 'Why don't they invent a gun with more slugs!' he demanded of Seven. 'Parkman got away!'

The outlaw got down from the bay and Seven managed to get the revolver out of his right holster and cock it. He pointed the gun at Flood as the outlaw came toward him.

Flood shook his head and a laugh came from deep within him. 'You are a real stubborn fella. Even while you're dyin' you keep up this prisoner-jailer business.'

'Am I dyin'?'

Flood knelt down before him and tore his shirt. 'No. We ain't goin' to let you die just yet. About four inches of ribs is exposed to the air. Burns' shot would have caught you dead center, except you went off your horse.'

'How 'bout my head?'

Flood said, 'Nothin'. Just messed up your hair, nicked you and put a hole in your hat. That was Ritter's shot.'

Flood got the bleeding stopped and Seven inched his way back to a rock to rest. 'It's a hell of a shock, gettin' shot.'

'Ain't it, though?' Flood got him some beef. 'Eat.'

'Where'd you get the gun?'

'Outa your left holster. I knocked you off your black and grabbed it about the same time.'

'I ain't gonna pass out,' Seven murmured. 'I ain't.'

Flood sat down near him and lit a cigar. 'Nobody said you was. I expect you to have this battleground cleaned up and be ready to move on before dark.'

# CHAPTER FIFTEEN

Five days later the two men, leading the two horses left over from the fight, rode across the Devil River where the Ranger camp had been, and headed toward Harrington's Trading Post.

After an hour, Seven shifted slightly in his saddle and worked the bandage around his chest to a more comfortable position beneath his underwear. 'We'll be gettin' there pretty quick.'

Flood nodded. 'So law an' order prevails again, and the world gets a little bit duller.'

The horses picked their way through a dry creek bed and clattered up the far side. Seven pulled his black to a halt under a ledge farther along and said, 'Stop a minute.'

'What for?'

Seven cocked his Colt and held the gun on the outlaw. Then he pulled his knife. 'I want to cut them ropes. I don't want the lieutenant to see you in 'em. Once he got that idea, he'd keep you in 'em forever.'

Seven pulled the knife blade through the binding cords and Flood rubbed his wrists. 'Feel like I already been in 'em forever.' He pushed his way back into a walk as Seven waved him ahead. 'Wish you'd decided to toss in with me as junior partner. We'd've cut a wide swath through the country.'

Putting his gun back once Flood was safely ahead of him, Seven said, 'We cut a fair-sized swath even so.'

'Yeah,' Flood agreed. 'We did, at that.'

It was quiet at the Trading Post and Ranger Head-quarters. Crossing the flats before the buildings, Seven kept a watch on the large building, hoping for a sight of Joy, aware that his heart was beating high in his chest. But neither she nor her father came into view. There were three horses tied before the reconverted chicken coop and the two

115

men swung down there and hitched their animals. A painted sign over the doorway said, 'COMPANY D, TEXAS RANGER FRONTIER BATALLION. *Captain Herly, C'md't.*'

Flood grinned. 'Herly's movin' up in the world.'

James came out of the door just before they got to it. 'Smith!' he yelped happily. 'Long time! Where's Hennesey?'

'Good t' see you, James. We can talk later.'

The two men went into the Ranger quarters and Seven nodded toward the office. Flood got there first and he swung the door open and went in.

Herly was at his desk. He glanced up with annoyance, and his mouth dropped open, then clamped shut.

Seven entered behind Flood and shut the door. 'I guess from the way you're lookin', that you know this is Jim Flood.'

Herly recovered quickly. 'Him and me have met before. Where's Hennesey, Smith?'

Seven had thought of a thousand things to say at this point. A thousand ways to dig at Herly, to show his bitterness and hate. But now none of them seemed to matter. None of them would do any good. He said simply, 'Dead. What's to be done with Mister Flood, Lieutenant?'

'We've got a cell at the other end of the building where you can put him. Sergeant Hoyt has the keys to it, and it's Captain now, Smith.'

'Oh, yeah. Noticed that on the door.'

Herly stood up. 'I guess you've been away long enough for me to overlook it this once, Smith. But you call me Sir.'

Seven said without anger, but flatly, 'That's your own rule. Not the Rangers'. Go to hell.'

There was a short silence and then Flood chuckled. 'I would bet a buck that's about exactly what Hennesey told this beanshooter of a Ranger.'

Herly's face was dark with anger. He stared from Flood to Seven. 'I'll expect a full report soon. Last word we had

116

from you was a note from Hennesey last fall. In the meantime, I'll notify Austin that I have Flood here.'

'Careful how you word that message, Herly,' Flood said. 'I'm here 'cause you sent two good men after me. But I ain't plannin' on staying long.'

Seven turned to the door. 'Shall we go on out, Flood?'

Hoyt and Carson were in the bunkroom beyond the door and Hoyt said, 'James said you was back, Seven. Welcome. This here big fella a guest?'

'Yes. Name's Flood. This, Flood, is Hoyt and Carson.'

'Wanna go in here, Flood?' Hoyt opened the thick oak door to the room sectioned off at the end of the building.

Flood went in and Hoyt turned a key in a large lock in the door. Seven couldn't take his eyes off the lock. It looked like the biggest, most solid lock in the world.

Carson crossed his arms over his chest and stared through the barred window in the door. 'Fancy introductions. And would you step in here, if ya' please? Just cause a man's been writ up some in the papers! He don't look nothin' special t' me, locked up in that cell.'

Seven said softly, 'You want a barrel bent over your head, Carson?'

'What?' Carson stepped away, surprised and indignant. 'You got no call t' be sore at me.'

'Watch out how you talk t' my prisoner.'

Seven went out a moment later to start stripping the horses, and Hoyt walked to the hitching rail. 'Lose Hennesey?'

'Yeh. In Utah.'

'You been quite a ways.' Hoyt pulled a splinter from the hitching rail and chewed on it thoughtfully, starring at Seven. 'Most a' the fellas you bring in are no damned good at all. No redeemin' qualities. I take it Flood is one of the other, rarer kind.'

'I think so.'

'When once in a great while that happens, it's like as if they was lockin' up part a' you with the man you brung in.

117

But you gotta remember you lost Hennesey on the trip. He was as good a man as I've known.'

Seven washed and shaved and then put on a clean shirt. He went to the cell door and looked inside. Flood was lying on the single bunk in the room, his hat over his eyes.

Seven said, 'I'll stop by from time to time and see if you're wantin' anything.'

'Okay. Good huntin' with the girl.'

Crossing the wide space between the Rangers' quarters and the trading post, Seven walked up the front steps to the gallery. He hesitated just a moment while crossing to the door, then went on in.

Joy was at the far side of the big room arranging some bolts of cloth on a shelf. She turned as she heard footsteps and her eyes grew big. 'Seven!'

He took off his hat and walked over to her. 'Just come in, maybe half an hour ago.' Glancing around the store, he said, 'Things look nice. Sure is nice to be back.' He looked into her large eyes and added, 'And you're looking prettier than I remembered you – which was pretty pretty.' And then he ran out of the words he was struggling to make up. 'Ain't you got nothin' to say?'

'Oh, Seven!' she whispered. 'We'd given you up for dead.'

'No, I ain't dead.'

'It's . . . nice to have you back!' She stepped forward and hugged him, smiling up at him with damp eyes. Then she called, 'Dad! Come see who's here!'

When Seven told Herly that he would be eating away from camp that night, the Captain nodded curtly and let it pass. Puzzled that the man had not argued the point, Seven brought it up over coffee with the Harringtons.

Joy said, 'He's known for some time now that any possible friendship between us is out of the question.'

Harrington put sugar in his coffee and stirred it slowly. 'Thing is, when the girl found out who he'd sent you after, she stopped speakin' to 'im in any way, shape or form. She ain't even looked his way in near a year now. Maybe he

118

figures you two seein' each other is no more concern of his.'

'I doubt it,' Joy said. 'He'll still be out to hurt Seven any way he can.'

Relaxing back in his chair, Harrington studied Seven with penetrating, kind eyes. 'You been gone the better part of a year, son. You've grown and filled in around the edges. There are some things you can't tell, and some things you won't tell – but aside from that, I'd like to hear you talk about the life you've lived in that time.'

After supper, sitting alone on the gallery with Joy, Seven said, 'One thing I've learned. A life can end awful quick. And too much of it is wasted. Foolin' around and not get-tin' to the heart of things. This is by way of saying that – I know I should see you a lot more before talkin' of it, but I'd be pleased and happy if I could have you as my wife.'

'A good courtship isn't a waste of time,' Joy said. 'But I'll consider you've already been at it for a year, even though you're not the best letter-writer I've ever heard of.' She smiled in the dark at him. 'And Dad's already called you son. He'll not be against the marriage.'

Later, when the moon rose over a line of hills in the northwest, a great glowing circle of silver, Joy whispered, 'What manner of man is Jim Flood? You speak of him with affection, yet he's done such terrible things.'

Seven was at a complete loss for words. He finally said, 'I don't know, Joy.' He thought a moment and then con-tinued. 'I can talk about 'im, all right, but I can't guarantee to make a clear picture of him. Maybe it sounds dumb, but he's kind of like the moon up there. Cold, but warm at the same time. Big. Alone. Over everythin' else. And the only one of his kind. I'd trust him with anything I had, knowin' at the same time he might turn on me at any minute.' He turned toward her. 'If the moon was a man, wouldn't you do that?'

Looking at the round globe in the sky, Joy leaned on Seven's shoulder. 'I don't know.'

'Flood is – independence, and doin' whatever you want to

do, and bein' able to do whatever you want to do, wrapped up in one man.'

'Yet they'll hang him.'

Seven thought about that. Then he said, 'I don't think so. If I'd really thought that, I doubt I coulda' brought him in.'


## CHAPTER SIXTEEN

Three days later Flood broke out.

It was early morning, before daylight, when it happened. The night before Seven had given the outlaw a handful of cigars. They'd talked briefly and Flood had grinned.

'You know, that Herly's got a real Indian glint in his eyes when he looks at your back.'

'He doesn't look too pleasant straight on, either.'

The first Seven knew of the break he was jarred out of his sleep by two thunderous roars that nearly busted his eardrums. He sat up in the dark along with the other Rangers in the room, and the door swept open and someone ran out.

'What'n the name a' God?' somebody shouted across the room. Most of the Rangers were yelling at once, and Seven drew on his boots as Hoyt struck a match to a kerosene lamp.

Several men piled outside along with Herley who came from his office wearing his guns strapped around his waist and hatless.

Seven glanced at the cell door as he got up. The door was open, the lock shattered, and Carson lay on his side on the floor with blood dripping from his mouth.

There was the sound of a gun roaring once from the barn behind the trading post, and within a few seconds another blast of pounding revolvers came from somewhere nearer. Then there was the swift, thumping, rhythm of a horse running and the noise of hooves was drowned out in a happy, ear-splitting warwhoop.

120

Taking his time, Hoyt hung the lantern from a hook and said, 'I'd say Flood ain't with us no more.'

A moment later, Rangers started pouring back into the room, pulling on boots and buckling on guns. They were all talking and yelling at once and Hoyt bellowed, 'Shut up!' The men quieted down and Hoyt turned to James, who had been one of the first men out. 'Where's Captain Herly?'

'Layin' out there, dead.'

'Flood's not human with a gun!' Priest said. 'Herly hadn't the chance of a snowball in hell!'

'Puts you in charge, Hoyt,' Jagers said.

Hoyt scratched his neck. 'Anybody got any idea how he got hold of a weapon?'

James muttered, 'He got Carson's gun. There's room t' reach out between them bars.'

'Yesterday,' Jagers added, 'Carson tol' me he was agoin' to come into a pile of money. Didn't say how.'

A Ranger named Begley rushed into the room. 'I run over t' the barn to see what the shootin' was there. Miss Harrington got shot!'

'Hit bad?' Hoyt demanded.

But Seven was gone before the man could answer. He raced across the open space leading to the barn and rushed into the big open structure with his lungs bursting. Harrington was in his undershirt and britches, leaning over Joy on the floor. Seven knelt down and saw that her eyes were open. He took her hand in both of his own, and Harrington said,

'She'll be all right, son. Bullet just flesh-hit her under the arm. I got the bleedin' stopped. She's kinda dazed, mostly.'

Seven scooped the girl up, noticing dimly that she weighed no more than a child, and carried her into the trading post while Harrington hurried ahead with a lamp.

Joy was starting to rest, her shallow wound cleaned and bound, when Hoyt came into the trading post and said, 'The rest of us are all set to go after 'im. I'm takin' the whole crew with me except you, Smith. I'm leavin' you here to

121

look after things.' He hesitated. 'She will be okay, won't she?'

'Looks that way.'

'So long.'

Joy was sleeping comfortably when Seven went back to Ranger quarters. Herly was laid out on his bunk in the office, and Carson had been placed on the floor beside him.

Seven spent the day at the trading post, and under his and Harrington's care, the girl came around and was eventually able to move by herself. Finally, around seven o'clock she went to sleep once more. And after talking to Harrington for a time, Seven started back toward the Ranger quarters. Night shadows had a firm grip on the countryside as he walked across the open land toward the long, low building.

He was a hundred feet from the door when he heard the sound of a single horse coming out of the distance in the night. Unhurriedly, he went on to the building. There were three double-barreled shotguns on a rack in the corner. He went to the corner in the dark and took down one of the scatterguns, breaking it open to make sure it was loaded, then snapping it shut.

He was on his way back to the door when the horse came to a halt in front of the building. Flood's voice called out softly, 'You there, Seven?'

'Yeah, I'm here.' Seven went out onto the dark ground beyond the door and could see Flood's dim figure leaning toward him from where he sat his horse a few feet away.

'Heard the girl got hit. It was dark in the barn. I just shot at a sound I heard.'

'Thought it was somethin' like that.'

'How is she?'

'Comin' along all right.'

Seven could make out the blurred, shadowy movement as Flood shifted weight on his horse and pulled his hat down a bit. 'I'm glad of it. Didn't want to ride on without tellin' you how it happened. That's the trouble with us devil-may-care fellas. Second time I've shot somebody I didn't want to. First Hennesey, and now her.'

'I guess that's why most men live pretty calm lives,' Seven said. 'There ain't a man wouldn't like to be like you. Free and wild and forever doin' as he pleases. But livin' that way, you're bound to hurt people – both meanin' and not meanin' to.'

'Yeah. It's a damn shame it has to be that way – Well, so long, Seven.' In the dark the outlaw pulled his mount's head up to turn and go.

'Flood! I want you to know somethin'.' Seven's voice caught slightly with feeling, then continued firm as the man on horseback hesitated. 'I want you to know that I think considerable of you, and think that you are about the best man I'll ever know.'

Seven swung the shotgun up quickly toward the figure in the night. Flood sensed the movement, the danger, and his gun was instantly in his hand. The revolver banged, and Seven felt a bullet rush by his head, heard the slug smack savagely into the building behind him.

And then, hard after the revolver shot, there were two immense, booming blasts that jarred the night air as Seven leveled the big gun, his thumb raking back the hammers, and shot both barrels at point blank range.

Seven's ears ached with the echo of the shotgun, and he realized the shooting was over. It could not have lasted more than a split second, but Seven could remember nothing in his life, for a moment, but standing in the dark and shooting at the shadowy image before him and the jet of fire leaping from Flood's gun. Then he knew the horse was running away, whinnying in terror, and that Flood had fallen to the ground.

Dropping his gun, Seven went to where there was a deeper shadow on the dark ground. 'Flood?' He got down on one knee and put his hand on the outlaw's chest. The chest was a mass of blood and torn flesh.

Flood said in a low voice, 'You learned to allow for your limitations as a gunfighter.'

123

'You still got off the first shot. You never missed such an easy shot. You pulled off.' Seven's voice was husky.

'At the last minute there,' Flood said slowly, 'I remembered you owe me eighty-five dollars – and I couldn't stand to lose that gamblin' debt.'

There was a faint, almost imagined sound that came through the dark in whispered softness to Seven's ears, and he realized that Flood had started a low, quiet laugh as he died. When it stopped, it was as though all the laughter Seven had ever known was stilled forever.

'Flood . . . Flood!' He tried to call him back, but it was no good.

Then Seven heard, as though from a great distance, a girl's voice crying his name, and Joy was at his side, sobbing with relief.

He stood up, taking her by the arm and raising her.

They started walking slowly back toward the trading post where Harrington was standing with a lamp held high in one hand and a rifle in the other.

THE END

# GUNSLINGER

He pulled the trigger as Boicourt's
revolver came free of leather. Boicourt was
thrown back against the bar by the
wallop of the heavy slug. He stared with
astonishment at Taw for a choking
moment, then slipped off the side.

The bartender hopped over the bar and
crouched down beside him. 'Dead',
he said quietly.

JACK TAWLIN was a living legend in a
land where gunmen died young. A man
marked for violence.

A man who dared a hold up nobody else had
the guts to try . . .

Also available in the
Huffaker Western series:
**FLAMING STAR**
**BADGE FOR A GUNFIGHTER**
**RIO CONCHOS**

# HUFFAKER

## BADGE FOR A GUNFIGHTER

## GAMBLING MAN

'I know a lot about you, Cash,' Whitey said. 'How you killed a man down in San Antonio and went on the prod. You've killed three men since'.

'Five', Cash said. 'Couple didn't get written up in the papers.'

'I like a man who hates people', Whitey said. That's a man you can count on. I'm making you sheriff of Yellowrock.'

For Cash shooting a man was just a matter of figuring the odds that he'd win and collecting the money he was paid for the killing. Now the sheriff's badge said he was the law. That made the odds in his favour a whole lot sweeter . . .